SLAVE RACE

BY

DWIGHT DALE MILLER

Paperback ISBN: 978-0-9984911-2-7
Ebook ISBN: 978-0-9984911-3-4

DEDICATION AND THANKS

This book is dedicated to all those with the courage to have made a commitment to follow their heart, no matter what.

"Two roads diverged in a wood, and I –

I took the one less traveled by,

And that has made all the difference."

~ A quote from Robert Frost's poem "The Road Not Taken"

I want to express my heartfelt love and gratitude to all those who have helped, guided, taught and inspired me, including Joseph Ghabi, Lorina Quigley, Dr. David Hawkins, Tom Bird, Dr. Roland Phillips and Cheryl Phillips, and Terri Tucker. Each of you has been a bright light to guide me far down the road less traveled. Thank you.

I love and appreciate my wonderful family and friends for all of your support. And to my amazing children: Tatum, Aubrey, Sydney and Billy, I love and appreciate you more than you can imagine. You have taught me far more than I have taught you. Thank you.

Table of Contents

CHAPTER 1

In this world, there is an incredible power that lies hidden in the shadows. I was born into such a family. My earliest memories do not consist of love, games or fun, but of the teachings. Early in life, I understood that in ancient Sumerian, the words "homo sapiens" meant "slave race." I was to be a master of the slaves.

After the age of two, I rarely saw my mother. She was from India, and remained at the family estate there, while my father and I spent most of our time at the coastal family estate near Los Angeles. Once a year I would visit the family estate in India, and I'd get to have lunch and dinner with my mother. I don't remember ever seeing my mother and father do anything together. I was always tended to by servants. From the age of three, I spent most of my time with one or two teachers each day.

My father was an American-born Englishman. He was handsome at five foot ten, thinly built, with jet-black hair, dark brown eyes and pasty-white skin. Fortunately, I got his height, build and hair, with slightly light-brown skin and

Mother's green eyes. My name, Nigel, was almost never spoken.

I was simultaneously taught my mother's Indian dialect and English, then later Mandarin and French. Learning these languages, especially how to read and write them, took up much of my time in my early youth.

I rarely ventured off the Los Angeles estate unless we were traveling by private jet to another family estate in southern England, outside Paris, in Hawaii or Hong Kong. There was always at least one security person with us wherever we went, and multiple guards always watched over each estate. Hong Kong, in particular, was well guarded.

When I did get a short break between studies, I enjoyed being outside on nice days. The warmth and liveliness of the outdoors was a refreshing change from the cold stone floors and the sounds of footsteps echoing far off down the vast halls. I enjoyed swimming lessons at age four, which were merely to ensure that I wouldn't drown in one of the estate's swimming pools, lakes or ponds. Once I learned to swim, I rarely got to swim for enjoyment, even though there was a heated pool in Los Angeles and many of the other estates.

"Your father is a very important man" is the most frequent thing I remember being told about him. "So, you are a very important boy," they continued. My father was a very strong person whose presence commanded absolute obedience. He gave instructions, and they were always followed without question. My inquisitive nature was quashed at a very young age when Father made it very clear that he didn't care about such feelings or questions. It was my duty to simply do what he said and learn my lessons.

"You have a soft side like your mother," I remember him telling me when I was four years old. "I should have chosen better." At first I thought it was a compliment, but the way he said it left me feeling confused. I wouldn't fully understand what he meant until much later.

The second thing I found joy in as a child was learning about animals. As part of my studies, I was to study all the different animals, including their behaviors and way of life, so that in my later lessons I would better understand the human slaves. These animal studies began at age five. At age seven, my teacher and a security guard would often take me on trips to zoos and aquariums. We would often sit there for several hours observing the same animals. At age eight, I went on my first of three African safaris.

Of all my lessons and experiences, traveling outside of the family estate to study the animals was by far the most enjoyable. The zoos and aquariums were public places, so I got to observe the slaves up close. The clothes they wore were appalling, yet they seemed to enjoy themselves at these places. Sometimes, while watching some of the animals, one of the children would actually say something to me. Until this time, I had never talked to another child. I acted and talked like an adult, so it was challenging to understand these children, though I was studying them intently. Of all the things I noted about the other children, the one thing that surprisingly stood out the most, was that they usually seemed happy. I hadn't expected that someone born into slavery would seem so innocent and happy.

I wouldn't have dared to ever say anything to Father about it, but deep inside I began to question how a child of slaves could be happier than I was. Instead of being with a teacher and a security person, they were with their parents, grandparents and often brothers or sisters. They played and had fun. They were so different than I was. Not only did they seem happy, but they were friendly toward me. One girl even asked me what my name was. No one had ever asked me that before. I didn't tell her. My interaction with them was incredibly awkward and adult-like, which often resulted in my seeing looks of confusion and disappointment on their faces. It was immediately obvious that I had a hard time being friendly and conversing with them.

Learning and studying the animals gave me a deep respect for nature and the natural order of things. Humans seemed so different. These first interactions with children kindled a deep, burning desire to learn more about the human slaves. When I turned eleven, new teachers arrived to help me study and learn about people. Also, for the first time, Father began to give me an occasional lesson himself. This was the first time he had ever spent any time with me, other than traveling in a car or plane together or sharing a rare meal.

After a month-long introduction to basic human psychology by a teacher, Father took me up in his helicopter on an unusually clear Los Angeles mid-spring Monday morning. I had felt so excited and important that Father was going to spend some time with me, I had barely slept the night before. He was a very busy and important man.

I was also excited for my first ride in the helicopter. My heart pounded with anticipation as we followed the security guard out of the rear entrance of the estate, then north through the gardens and the huge lawn. The sun warmed my skin while the ocean breeze felt cold on my nervous, sweaty palms. My impatience wondered why we hadn't taken the car, but at long last we arrived at the helipad, which was about fifty feet from the top of the cliffs overlooking the deep blue ocean as far as I could see.

The guard first went to the pilot's side and opened the door for Father, then he came around and opened the door for me. He helped me strap in while Father turned the power on and checked all the gauges and information on the front panel. The guard shut the helicopter door and walked away. Once he was far enough away, the helicopter's rotor blades fired up and began to whirl above us. Soon, my heart jumped and my stomach sank as we lifted off the ground, then tilted forward and over the sea cliff. I felt like I was strapped into a giant flying fish bowl with all the glass around me. It was both scary and exhilarating. Below us, the ocean waves crashed and splashed high upon the rocks as we began to climb and fly away. I beamed a huge smile as we lunged forward, sinking back into my seat as we accelerated rapidly.

I looked over to say something to Father, but he looked focused. Father was always serious. A few more minutes passed and we were flying over the ocean near a beach. Father handed me a pair of binoculars.

"What do you see?" Father asked.

"It's a beautiful day," I answered.

"Yes, yes," he responded. "But I want you to focus on the people this morning. Most of your lessons now will be about people. What do you see?" he inquired again.

"I don't see very many people," I answered.

"Yes. Tell me more about those that you do see," he instructed.

I looked closer and said, "Some are running or exercising. Some are walking. I see four in the water."

"Yes. Tell me more about those that you see running, walking or in the water," he prodded.

I said, "I see four people running. Three are men and one is a woman. There are six people walking along the ocean's edge. One man, one woman, and then two pairs of a man and a woman. They are much older than the ones running. The four in the water are playing in the waves. Three are surfing and one is boogey-boarding."

Father responded, "Yes. That is more of the kind of answer I am looking for. Do these people look good or bad? Do they look happy or sad?"

I zoomed in to look at them. I could not see all of their faces from where we were. I said, "The ones that I can see their faces, I think they look good. They seem happy or at least peaceful."

"Excellent," replied Father. "Now look at how dense the housing is in this area. Don't you see mostly houses, apartments and condominiums? How many houses do you think you can see?"

"Hmmm. Yes, there are many places to live here. Hundreds and hundreds, probably thousands of them," I answered.

Father replied, "It's such a beautiful morning. People live right next to this beach in nearly every residence you can see right now. Why aren't they outside enjoying the beautiful morning?"

"I don't know," I answered. "Maybe they are all still asleep?" I guessed.

"That is a good guess," he answered. "There is more to see this morning. Keep studying everything that you see." The helicopter climbed higher as Father steered over the shore toward the tall buildings in the city. A couple of minutes passed before he asked again, "What do you see?" We were above an intersection of major freeways.

"All the roads are full of cars," I answered. I looked in every direction: north, south, east and west. One of the freeways had eight lanes going each way. The others had six lanes. As far as I could see to the horizon, every lane of these wide freeways was jam-packed with cars that were barely moving. Their red brake lights formed laser-like lines to the horizon.

"Yes. Do the people look happy or sad?" he asked.

I zoomed into each car through the binoculars. The answer was obvious. I searched car after car, looking for an anomaly. After peering into several dozen cars, I gave up on finding the anomaly and answered decisively, "No one looks happy."

"Yes. Where is everyone going?" he asked.

I searched for an answer. "I don't know," I responded.

Father expected my response. "They are all going to work," he said plainly. Then he asked, "From all of your animal studies, does what you see down there remind you of anything?"

This answer was also obvious. "Ants," I responded. "Long lines of ants out to forage for food to bring back to the queen."

"Exactly, my son," Father responded looking pleased, which surprised me. "All of these people, millions of them in just Los Angeles today, are ants going to work, and their work benefits us. In the world, there are over seven billion ants. We are the queens of these ants."

Father let that soak in for a while as we soared over the city's glimmering tall buildings and its clogged freeways. Then he asked, "Why do you think all of these people are sitting in their cars, not happy, going to work, when they could be on the beach enjoying this beautiful morning?"

I struggled to find the answer. I could not imagine why anyone would possibly want to sit in their car all that time, and not look happy, and go to work, when they could be enjoying the beautiful day on the beach. "I don't know, Father," I answered. "Is it because they are slaves?" I asked.

Father laughed at my innocence. I still can picture this memory so clearly, like it happened just a moment ago. It was the first time I remember seeing my father laugh and smile. Then he said, "You will learn, my son. And when you fully understand this, you too, will be a master of the slaves."

CHAPTER 2

The human slaves absolutely fascinated me. So much of their behavior seemed impossible for me to understand, which fueled a volcano of desire for me to learn more. There was so much to learn. When I turned eleven, two new teachers came in to educate me on the human slaves. The first teacher focused on teaching me how the average American lived in their daily life. The second teacher began to teach me about the family business.

To learn about how the average American lived, the first thing I was shown was television and movies. Until this point, I had never watched a television program or movie. I had seen televisions in passing when I visited the zoos, aquariums and museums. I learned that the average American spent nine to ten hours every day watching television, movies and social media. "If they watch these things for nine or ten hours a day, how do they get anything done?" I asked.

"They don't," was the simple response from my middle-aged blonde teacher. Her straight hair was pulled tightly back into a bun. She always wore a nice black or navy dress, matching high heels and black-rimmed glasses. She looked very smart. "Most of them go to school or work, and then this is how they spend most of their time in between. We get them addicted to being stimulated all the time, so they feel they need to always be plugged in."

For a whole two weeks, I studied some of the most popular television and movie programs. I started by watching the most popular shows that the youngest children watched. It shocked me. There was so much violence, even death in some of these animated movies and shows. It was hard for me to watch. My teacher pointed out to me how many of these things were by design. I watched how the prince and the money were set up to be powerful and desirable, and how the women all swooned and wanted him and his wealth. These women were all perfectly beautiful, thin and yet voluptuous. From the earliest ages, the human slaves were being programmed to desire wealth, power, sex, beauty and nice things. Not only that, but they were being desensitized to violence.

I also paid attention to all of the commercials. The younger audiences were bombarded by things to buy, or what my teacher called "objects of desire." The themes of desire, sex, beauty, power and wealth were amplified for the older audiences. I looked at all the wealth surrounding me and I saw all the things positioned in the movies and television programs as objects of desire.

The worst part of my training by far was that I watched all the news programs for an entire day. I had never imagined that so much death, destruction, conflict, evil or sad events could occur in the world. And this was just in one day! It really affected me. I felt sick to my stomach for most of the day. When I asked how people could tolerate watching the news, I was simply told, "They are desensitized to it. This is all part of the design. For them, this is normal. We show them things to fear. Then we continually feed those fears. A good example is in our governments: we always create an enemy so that people will rally behind the government. The slaves are easily motivated by fear. Perception of peace is bad for business."

There was almost nothing that I watched in those two weeks of watching television and movies that I saw any value in, except for some of the comedies. I did get some laughs from a couple of shows, but other than that, I could not believe that people spent nine or ten hours a day watching such garbage. "No wonder they are slaves," I thought to myself.

Then I was given a one-day introduction to social media, including Facebook, Twitter and Instagram. This gave me insight into what the slaves actually focused on in their daily lives. I could see what they were talking about. My teacher instructed me to ask myself if each post was negative or positive or happy or sad. So many of the posts were focused on problems, negative news events or other things. It was starting to depress me, until I remembered that all these people were slaves. The one category I found to be positive was those artists and photographers who shared their art, and I liked some of the posts about animals. There were some beautiful creations, and amazing photos and stunning scenery. But these positive things were by far the minority.

After two weeks with my first teacher learning about how the American slaves spent their day, my second teacher arrived. These two teachers would spend a lot of time with me over the next few years. The second teacher was a small, wise-looking Chinese man with greying hair. His lessons focused on the family business, which included various family enterprises and government. I was sitting with my pen and notebook on the dark leather couch in the main living room as he sat down on the leather chair to my left. "So, you have seen what many Americans focus their attention on, yes?" he asked.

"Yes," I replied. "Almost all of it is total garbage."

He answered with a nod, "Yes. We human beings are very easily influenced. Particularly when young, humans accept everything as the truth and question very little. So by design, we bombard them with images of perfection, with themes that they need objects, beauty and wealth to be happy. They soak up this information for ten hours every day, starting from when they are very young. Today, I will start to show you how this translates into their behavior related to our businesses."

He continued, "The first thing you must understand is that there is a grand illusion portrayed to the slaves. They believe many things, all because they are never shown anything that contradicts any of these things. Men like your father, in just thirteen families across the world, are the real source of power and the creators of the illusion that the slaves live in."

The teacher continued, "Nelson Rockefeller once said publicly, "The secret to success is to own nothing, but control everything." This is exactly what the super-wealthy do. There are legal entities, mostly LLCs and corporations, that carry out the interests of these powerful men. There are typically layers of men between the powerful family and the entity, as well as layers of entities owning other entities, so that the powerful people can remain hidden. This also hides and protects these families' wealth. In the United States, for example, many of the organizations that people think are parts of the government are actually corporations controlled by us."

"Have you ever wondered why we do not use names here? I am sure you have noticed this, but you may not yet understand how extremely unusual this is. Most of the world interacts freely using their names. Here, we are secretive. We do not need to impress anyone with who we are. We are what we are, and we are better off not drawing attention to ourselves." He paused for a moment as he studied me. "Do you have any questions?" he asked.

"I don't really understand the legal things you're discussing, but I understand the goals of such things. I think I am good so far," I answered.

"Excellent," he replied. Then he asked me a fascinating question, "If you had billions and billions of dollars, and you networked with the other families who had similar wealth, what things would you want to control?"

I felt my brain rev up to process this question. At eleven years old, I did not yet understand how the various things in our society worked. "I am sure I would want to control many things, whatever I could. I do not know what they are yet. You mentioned the government already."

He smiled patiently at my response, then said, "Think about the biggest things and where the power is." He paused as he watched my wheels spinning, then said, "Government is where the power is. These decisions determine how all the government's money is spent, how people's income is taxed, what industries are favored vs. unfavored. Like a great puppet master behind the scenes, we control what the government officials do."

He continued, "Banks hold all the money. You may have noticed that in many cities, the biggest and tallest buildings are often those of banks. If you and your friends controlled much of the wealth in the world, you would definitely want to control the banks."

My lightbulb was turning on. "Oil!" I said proudly, remembering the incredible wealth of all the old oil barons, the oil wealth in the Middle East, and picturing all the cars and airplanes burning fuel around the world.

"Exactly," he agreed. "Controlling energy is an incredible source of power. In addition, think how much money it takes to build an electrical network for a city, or a network of roads and railroads across the country. Can you think of things that people consume every day? Electricity and gasoline are great examples."

"Food?" I asked without confidence. He nodded yes. "Water!" I exclaimed confidently.

"Yes!" he said. "Water is a great example to talk about. Water is the next oil. In many parts of the world, water is becoming polluted. Clean water is becoming scarce; therefore, it is becoming more valuable. Over the last decade, the super-wealthy began investing heavily in water. Do you think it's a coincidence that not much seems to be getting done about water pollution while the wealthy invest in water?"

"No," I answered as I shook my head as I thought about it. I had never made the connection before.

"Is there anything else?" he asked with his keen dark eyes fixed upon me.

I answered, "For sure the media, as it has already been mentioned. I can see how television, social media, movies and everything else create the illusion that the slaves live in."

"Absolutely," he acknowledged. "The invention of television, computers, the internet and now social media allow us to create and reinforce whatever illusion we desire. It's so easy now. If someone posts an opposing view on social media, we simply delete it or filter it out from what others will see. We control the internet. The masses swim in our messaging for ten hours per day, following our illusion like lemmings to the sea."

"Pay attention to this next point. This is probably the most critical tactic in our business. There are always a few who question things, but our strategy is to always divide the slaves so that they fight among themselves. Our politician puppets and media are masters at this. The slaves spend so much time focused on fighting each other that they do not see us, though in many ways we are in plain sight." I nodded my head as the news programs I had watched scrolled through my mind

"Can you think of anything else right now?" he asked. I searched my mind for a while before I gave in and shook my head and said, "No."

"Very well," he responded. "There are four other major areas worth mentioning right now, though as you can imagine, the super-wealthy influence many areas in many ways."

"Another major industry is what I'll simply call the war industry. This largely overlaps with our government business due to the colossal annual spend of the American government, but also includes guns and ammunition that we supply around the world. You can look at countries in Africa where people don't have money for food or medicine, but we're able to sell assault rifles and ammunition to militant groups via government funding. The war industry is a huge business, so our puppet government officials ramp up the war mongering to keep the cash flowing in. There's nothing like a good war to use up inventory of bombs, guns, bullets and equipment so that we can sell more to the government. Of course the families make money from both sides of the war."

"Next is healthcare and pharmaceuticals. America is the paradise of profit for healthcare. We charge Americans the highest prices in the world for prescriptions and services, and since healthcare here is for-profit, we can raise rates and deny services whenever we see fit. This business is a juggernaut cash cow as the health of Americans continues to decline. Over one hundred years ago now, we took over the education and regulation of doctors and healthcare providers. Back then, we virtually eliminated all of the natural-healing modalities. We shut down natural remedies and created drugs to be used in their place."

"Fifty years ago, we began steering the population to eat a high-carbohydrate diet. The body processes carbs like sugar. Sugar feeds disease. Did you know that in the body, cancer cells are among the first to feed off sugar? Doctors inject a radioactive substance with sugar to identify where cancer is in the body. Our brains are made of fat, so this low-fat and low-cholesterol diet starved the slaves' brains. This keeps the slaves weak, and now you see a spike in Alzheimer's and other mental disorders."

"Today, doctors are our drug dealers. Over fifty-five percent of Americans take pharmaceuticals, averaging four different drugs each. One in six women take anti-depressants to cope with depression, anxiety, stress, the realization that they married a dud or a jerk, or that they are not living their life purpose. These drugs keep them complacent, right where we want them. The slaves take these drugs every day, creating a huge income stream for us. We sell them insurance that gives them a big discount on these drugs, but at the same time we have rocketed the drug prices that are paid by the insurance companies. Then every year we raise the insurance prices, often by ten percent or more. It's beautiful."

"Unseen by many, we also pump a huge supply of pharmaceuticals into livestock that produce dairy and meat. The term "cash cow" rings very true here.'

"Starting when they are born, we pump multitudes of toxins into the slave children via vaccinations, which we've been able to multiply over recent decades even without any major health epidemics. When people eventually get sick, and most of them will, we are able to extract huge chunks of

21

wealth from them via the healthcare system. There are over three hundred twenty-seven million people in the U.S. Nearly half of its senior citizens die with less than ten thousand dollars in the bank. We bleed them dry." He smiled widely, and I couldn't help but grin when I thought about all this money. Three hundred million ants in America alone, who worked all of their lives for us. It seemed so easy.

The teacher continued, "All of these pharmaceutical drugs are chemicals entering the slaves' bodies. Most drugs simply minimize the symptoms experienced without addressing the actual cause of the health condition. These chemicals often generate side effects, and may accumulate in the body over a longer time period manifesting other health conditions. Fortunately for us, some of these drugs are quite addictive."

"Somewhat related is the alcohol industry. Alcohol is a drug that is very addictive. It is a very effective neurotoxin that affects the brain, nervous system and liver. Just like I mentioned with the anti-depressant drugs, many slaves consume alcohol to escape the reality of their daily life. Due to our ever-consistent messaging, they also associate alcohol with fun and sex. Some of them even believe studies that say consuming up to two glasses of this neurotoxin per day is good for them. Now, across the U.S., marijuana is being legalized. These drugs keep the slaves in altered states, disempowering them. Right where we want them."

The teacher continued, "Another critical industry we control is the education system. Just like our control of the media, the control of education keeps the young slaves focused on what we want them to focus on, without introduction of alternative ideas. We intentionally keep education under-invested in and pay teachers poorly to discourage the brighter slaves from teaching. The American educational system has barely advanced in the last fifty years."

"Here's one of my favorite examples for the importance of the educational system to our business. Many years ago, we invented the concept of inflation and taught this to all the slaves. The underlying concept behind inflation is that the price of something is expected to increase every year. The media reports inflation indexes, reinforcing to the slaves that prices are indeed increasing all the time. Today, the slaves all believe in the fact that they will pay more for the same exact thing this year than they did last year. So we just keep raising prices on everything in our businesses. Even if a slave gets an annual pay increase at their job, they just wind up paying most of it to us through higher prices on all the things they buy."

The teacher added, "Last for today is the chemical industry. Much of the chemical usage goes unseen. Every piece of clothing worn by a slave, every bed sheet, linen, piece of furniture, carpet or fabric in the household, work environment or car is treated with fire retardant. Farmers spray anti-pest and anti-weed chemicals on their crops of grains, fruits and vegetables. Chemicals are added to food as preservatives, flavor enhancers, sugar substitutes, etc. Chemicals are added to shampoo, soap, lotions, deodorant, etc. Fluoride and other chemicals are added to the water. People are literally swimming non-stop in chemicals, and they wonder what makes them sick. Your father is one of the largest forces in chemicals. A great river of cash flows into his bank accounts non-stop. Some of the same companies that make the chemicals that make people sick are the same ones that develop pharmaceuticals. Isn't that interesting?"

I simply nodded my head up and down as I stared at the floor in front of us. My thoughts were swirling.

"I can see you have enough to think about for a while," he said with a light chuckle and smile. "I will walk you through some more high-level details, and then we will break for lunch. Over the next few years, I will teach you in full detail about all of these things. Your father wants you to be ready to take over for him when the need arises."

The chef had prepared one of my favorites for lunch: grilled salmon, roasted vegetables and garlic mashed potatoes. I ate outside on the covered patio, overlooking the sparkling light-blue pool and the deep-blue ocean, as the gentle, salty breeze blew through my hair and cleared my mind. I wanted to learn all these lessons and I knew I had no choice, but part of me wanted to take surfing lessons and play on the beach. It had been years since I had asked Father for any such thing. I knew what the answer would be. Was I willing to take the risk and ask him? I pondered this just for a minute; then it was time to continue my lessons and practice speaking Mandarin.

When I arrived back in the living room, my teacher was waiting patiently for me. "I have good news for you," he announced. "I just received a message from your father. He is returning from his travels and will be here around the time you and I finish today's lesson. He wants to speak with you about the importance of these lessons."

"OK. Great!" I said quickly, trying to act excited. I thought to myself nervously, "Here's my chance to ask about surfing lessons."

The teacher continued, "He also spoke to me about the time he took you up in the helicopter. He asked if I could give you some understanding of why so many people choose to go to work instead of enjoying the beach. This is a wonderful place to start, as it will tie in some of the things we covered before lunch."

He explained, "The first thing you need to understand is that nearly everything costs money. So, if the human slave desires a lot of things, and/or very expensive things, they will need a lot of money to buy and maintain these things. Remember how all of the images and advertisements appealed to their desires?"

"Yes," I replied knowingly.

He continued, "So, the human grows up and wants this and wants that. Nearly all of them receive no education about money or budgeting. That is also by design. As soon as they turn eighteen years old, if they are in college or working, they start getting offers to borrow money with credit cards or car loans. We make it extremely easy for them to borrow money. Most of them will accept some or all of these offers so that they can fulfill their desires immediately, instead of saving up and paying cash for the objects of their desire. This puts them in debt, and from this point forward, for most of them their future as a slave is already certain."

"For example, say someone wants to buy a car that costs twenty thousand dollars. Most new cars are far more expensive than this, but we'll use twenty thousand as an example. The person doesn't have twenty thousand dollars in the bank. They only have two thousand. They pay their two thousand dollars down and borrow eighteen thousand so they can buy the car. They not only have to make payments to pay back the eighteen thousand dollars, but they also have to pay interest on the loan. If it's a five percent loan, they pay an extra five dollars per year for every hundred dollars they borrow. You don't need to understand the exact math right now, but do you understand this so far?"

"Yes," I nodded.

He continued, "This car loan forces the person to make payments for, let's say, three hundred dollars per month for the next six years. Plus, they will likely pay over two hundred dollars per month for car insurance. Now let's say they also want nice clothes and things in their house or apartment, so they borrow money using a credit card. That creates more debt and the interest rates are much higher, often above twenty-five percent."

"Listen closely to this point. This is the key. The willingness to go into debt is all created by their insatiable desire. They want nice things to make them feel good. They think that if they have these things and look successful, they will attract an attractive lover. So sexual desire is also a big motivator. Again, we make it extremely easy for them to borrow money. Often. loan approval happens within just a few minutes."

"Many of them will go to college and borrow over one or two hundred thousand dollars in college loan debt, which they have to pay back plus interest. Since the government backs student loans, colleges are able to charge aggressive tuition rates, which means more debt for the students. When the slaves get out of college, many of them will buy a home – and they borrow hundreds of thousands of dollars to do that. The monthly payments on all these debts add up to thousands of dollars. Even when they pay off a car loan, most of them will turn around and buy a newer car and start a new car loan. Do you see how, based on their own choices, they sign themselves up for a lifetime of work?"

"Yes," I said. "It's all starting to make sense. They enslave themselves."

"Exactly," agreed the teacher. "The banks, owned by the wealthy, just make the loans and collect the interest. The workers work to pay off their debt, and in doing so, create more profits for the companies they work for."

"I see," I said. "It was amazing to see how many people were traveling to work all at one time. As far as I could see in any direction, the freeways were jammed with cars. How do the slaves not see this?"

"Go back to what I said were the keys," he reminded me. "From the earliest ages, they are bombarded with images of the reality we want them to live in. They are never shown anything else. Within them, we create an insatiable desire for objects. Almost all of them take this path, so it is accepted as the normal way to live. Most of them do not even question it, or when they do, it is too late."

"I like this lesson very much," I admitted. "Studying the human slaves is really fascinating, much more so than the animals. The animals are much smarter."

The teacher chuckled at this. "Indeed. This is a good point to end this lesson today. Let's take a ten-minute break, and then we'll practice your Mandarin."

It was nice to have someone to converse with in Mandarin. It had been a while. We spoke back and forth, with him correcting me here and there, for the next hour and a half. Then Father arrived, and I got up to greet him.

"Hi, Son," he said in his business-like voice as he walked up to me.

"Hi, Father," I said warmly.

He turned to my teacher and asked, "How was today's lesson?"

"Excellent," he replied. "He is starting to gain an understanding of why so many humans must go to work, and some of the ways we do things."

"Perfect," Father replied. "You may go now," he instructed the teacher with a wave of his hand to leave our presence. The teacher bowed and left quickly, then Father turned to me.

"These new lessons are very important. You will gain an understanding that very few in the world possess. Do not take them lightly. Come. There is something I want to show you," as he gestured for me to follow him.

"Yes, Father," I replied as I followed him. We walked out of the main living room, through an adjacent room, and then another until we came into the main hallway to the southern wing of the house. There were several old oil paintings on the wall, featuring groups of men, which I had never paid much attention to. Father turned to me and looked me in the eyes as he said, "I call this the hall of kings," as he gestured to each of the paintings.

He explained further as he pointed to an old map on the wall, "Only one hundred years ago, the British Empire covered nearly one fourth of the world's geography and population. These men you see here are our great forefathers. They were great men, conquerors, and creators of massive empires. They sailed across oceans in wooden ships, landed on foreign soil and dominated entire civilizations. It is these men who created the kingdom you and I now enjoy. It is our great duty and honor to continue in their spirit."

He went to the first oil painting, which, like the others, illustrated a dignified-looking group of white men in the front with brown-skinned native-looking people in the background. One of the natives, who also looked important, was dressed like the British. Father explained that the most prominent British man was our relative, and he told me of the man's great accomplishments. He did the same with the other five paintings. For over two hundred years, our forefathers were a prominent part of the British Empire.

"Wow. I had no idea," I admitted. I was impressed.

He was invigorated as he continued, "Once you have more money than you will ever possibly need, the only remaining challenge is the pursuit of power. Sometimes, I am jealous of the good old days, when a man could simply take whatever he was capable of taking in plain daylight. You could just take the men and women. You could take them as slaves. If you wanted a woman, you took her. If someone got in your way, you just beat or killed him. Some things are easier to do in India and some corners of the world, but it's harder everywhere else. I think about how well our system works today, where people enslave themselves. It's too easy. It just doesn't seem as satisfying," he concluded intensely, as a thick vein bulged down his forehead

Everything felt surreal as I contemplated his words and silently nodded my head, but all I could think was, "So much for surfing lessons."

CHAPTER 3

All the lessons I started at age eleven continued over the next three years in great detail. I learned how the super-powerful families acted like master puppeteers, faking elections, buying or otherwise influencing politicians and leaders of business, banking, major industries, entertainment, news and social media. Their influence was everywhere.

My lessons in understanding how people lived in their daily lives were extended outside of America. I traveled extensively during these years with my teachers and a security guard. I was shown the wealthiest and poorest parts of countries including Mexico, India, China, the U.S., the U.K., France, Germany, Greece, the Czech Republic, Turkey, Egypt and South Africa. We stayed longer in India, China and France so that I could immerse myself further in those languages. All the countries had wonderful parts, and all of them had absolutely terrible parts. It was an eye-opening experience.

Among the more advanced nations, it really stood out to me how many people in the U.S. were homeless. It's simply something I never saw in the parts of Europe that I had visited. There was so little support for them in the U.S. compared to the European countries I had visited. But compared to the poor in the poorest of areas in India and China, the homeless in the U.S. were living well. In the poorer countries, people were literally starving to death and/or living in garbage dumps.

I had lived most of the time on the coastal estate outside of Los Angeles. I eventually realized one other significant thing about the U.S. compared to other countries. Compared to the U.S., a family could be really poor in India, Mexico or China, for example. But what surprised me was that they could also be fairly happy. In many cases, they seemed happier than the average American, even though in terms of wealth or quality of life they possessed far less than the American. Americans were the most engrossed in slavery, so focused on work and money compared to people in these other countries. The foreigners worked, but they did not live for work. It was very noticeable. This also reminded me of my earliest experiences with the other children at the zoos and aquariums, and how those children seemed happier than I was.

I enjoyed these few years of lessons and travel, which passed by quickly. At age fourteen, a new level of learning began. A wise man from India was brought into Los Angeles to teach me these special lessons. Father told me that very few people on the planet, especially in the western hemisphere, understood what I was about to learn. He called these lessons "the keys to the kingdom." He said that it would explain why what we did was so effective. I was intrigued.

The Indian teacher and I sat outside on the back patio in the shade. The thin little old gray-haired man smiled. He was friendly, but he was missing two of his front teeth: one on the top right side and one on the bottom left, which I found quite disturbing. The very first lesson got my attention right away. "What are you?" he asked.

"What do you mean?" I asked. "What am I?" I repeated out loud in wonder, asking him if that was really the question.

"Just answer the question," he persisted. "What do you think you are?"

"OK," I said slowly, thinking this was a total waste of time. "I'm a fourteen-year old boy. A human being. A future master of slaves." I looked at him, thinking that this was an adequate response.

"What does it mean to be a boy, to be a human being?" he asked.

"Oh my God," I thought to myself. "What the hell have I gotten myself into? Is Father playing some kind of practical joke on me?" I wondered if he had found out I had watched some online porn videos and this was his way of torturing me. I sat there staring blankly at the old teeth-missing man.

He smiled and sat there patiently, waiting for me to answer. "I don't know how to answer you," I confessed.

He helped me out a little, "When you see yourself as a boy, what do you see?"

I replied, "Hmmm. OK. I see my body, arms, legs, stomach, back, etc. Inside I have a brain, a heart, blood, bones, organs, etc."

"Interesting," he replied as he continued to stare at me. At one point I waved my hand across my body, as it seemed like he was looking at me, but he wasn't looking at ME. I don't know how to explain it. He just sat there for a while longer. Finally, he asked, "Do you think you are just like any other animal then?"

I thought about this for a few seconds and then replied, "Yes. I suppose. Just smarter, and able to do more things because of my hands, opposable thumbs, etc."

Then he held up his right hand with his palm facing toward me about five feet away. He just held it there. And the weirdest thing happened. I could feel something hitting my forehead, something kind of flowing. "What is that?" I asked as I rubbed my forehead.

"What is what?" he replied.

"I feel something on my forehead," I answered.

"That is a very good sign," he said as he smiled encouragingly. "What you feel hitting you is called prana in India. It is energy." I sat there baffled. I had no idea what to do with what he had just told me.

"The animal-like characteristics you just described to me, that is indeed what you see. But it is not the most significant part. You are so much more." He paused as he continued staring in my direction. I just sat there, now more attentively. Then he continued, "While in the womb, often near four months old, the soul comes in and joins with the body." He paused again, studying me, then asked, "So, do you think you are the body, this animal, or something much more?" He could tell he had my attention. I could not answer him. I had heard the word soul before, but I had no idea what it meant.

Then he said, "Every human has the same condition. We have two masters that we may serve. One is the animalistic ego. Like the animal, it is the senses and the body that you described. It is also the brain and its mental logic, the hormones, the adrenaline and the emotions. It experiences fear in the form of fight or flight; it desires money, objects, sex and power; it experiences guilt, shame and hate; and it judges others. It is always self-serving and focused on its survival, just like an animal. Does this make sense so far?" he asked. I nodded my head up and down.

He continued, "The other master is the soul. It is eternal. It is pure energy and resides in the heart area. Only good things resonate from it, though you may also have stored fear and other emotions near your body's heart, which is not of the soul. The soul only emanates love, joy, peace, compassion, all of these higher states."

"This is interesting, but I'm not sure what I'm supposed to do with it," I told him. I had become much more confident and outspoken at age fourteen.

"Patience is often not an attribute of the young," he remarked. Then he explained further, "Think about all that you have learned about influencing the behavior of the people. What I am going to teach you, if you are open to it, is simply a higher level of understanding. If you want to keep people down in lower levels of consciousness, you drive them to focus on the characteristics of the animalistic master. Have you learned anything yet about levels of consciousness?" he asked.

"No. I have never heard of that," I replied. "It sounds cool, though," I admitted.

He smiled at my response. "I will give you a brief overview of the basics. We will explore all of these concepts in great depth over the next year. If you haven't heard of chakras, you have seven major chakras from the base of your spine to the top of your head. At the bottom is the root chakra. It relates to survival issues, and to fear of lacking basic necessities like health, food, safety, etc. It points downward from the perineum area." He pointed his right index finger down from his crotch to illustrate. "It's associated with the color red. So a person who experiences fight or flight, or panic, for example, has issues with their root chakra. Got it?" he asked.

"Yes," I confirmed.

He continued, "The five middle chakras are on both your back and front. The second chakra is the sacral chakra, which is two finger-widths below your belly button. Its energy relates to connections with others, communication, sex and reproduction, and it has a great influence over creativity. I can see your energy has been building up in this area, which is normal for a teenage boy. Its color is orange."

"The third chakra up the spine is the solar plexus chakra. On the front, you can find it located in the soft area just beneath the center of your rib cage. This is a great source of will and power. It can give a person the willpower to overcome obstacles and accomplish great things. Symptoms of a weak solar plexus chakra are lack of motivation, depression. These people will not be able to accomplish things or stand up for what they believe in. This chakra can also feed a person's desire for power and control over others. Its color is yellow. Make sense?" he asked and paused for me to catch up with writing my notes.

Then he said, "The fourth chakra is the heart chakra at the center of the chest. It is the great doorway to the higher levels of consciousness. Love lives here, along with fear, and feelings of hurt and heartbreak. There are usually many obstacles between the solar plexus and heart chakra that one must overcome to reach the level of the heart chakra. Its color is green."

"From the heart chakra and higher, a person's focus becomes more on others than on themselves. They focus on the benefit of all. The most inspiring leaders in history were able to speak from their heart and appeal to these higher states of being. But there probably hasn't been such an inspiring, prominent leader in America since JFK or MLK, over fifty years ago. Most of today's leaders are motivated solely by power and greed, so they play their roles well for us."

"The fifth chakra is the throat chakra, at the bottom of your throat, and it is associated with your voice and other means of expression. An open throat chakra enables one to speak their truth through your voice, writing, art or way of life. Its color is blue."

"The sixth chakra is the "third eye" or brow chakra, located between your eyebrows. It is a great source of intuition and psychic power. Some people can literally see energy and other things that human eyes do not typically see. Clairvoyance can be attained through the third eye. Its powers can also be used to manipulate the thoughts of others. Its color is indigo."

"The seventh and last chakra is the crown chakra at the very top of your head. It emanates upward. It is the connection to the divine, your soul, and other higher-level beings, and therefore, knowledge. Its energy is violet. Have you ever wondered how ancient societies did things that today's society, with all of its advancements in technology, cannot figure out?"

"Yes!" I exclaimed. "I am fascinated by ancient Egypt's pyramids and places like Stonehenge and Machu Picchu."

"The answer is quite simple," he replied with an easy, teeth-missing smile. "Those people were able to access higher levels of knowledge. The knowledge did not come FROM them. It came THROUGH them."

"This guy is freakin' weird!" I thought to myself. "And I love it."

The teacher continued, "You can remember the colors of the chakras by "ROY-G-BIV," which follow the same exact pattern as a rainbow. This is important: each successive chakra and color is higher in frequency, energy and vibration. As one's focus in life moves up the chakras, so does the person's energy, vibration and personal power." Every person has the potential to tap this incredible power. He paused as I scrambled to catch up on my notes. "Does this make sense?" he asked.

"It does," I replied.

"Very good," he said. "Now, to your earlier question of what this knowledge is useful for, do you have a better idea now?"

"Well, more knowledge, energy and power sound good," I said. "Other than that, I'm not sure yet," I admitted.

"All journeys start with the first step, yes?" he asked.

"Yes," I agreed.

"Our goal is very simple. Keep the people in the lowest chakras. This keeps them weak and self-centered, so they will not be able to rise up against us. If they think life is hard, if they struggle, if they live in fear, if they worry about their health, safety, putting food on the table and paying their bills, then the focus of their life will be in the root chakra. This is why the news and media focus on all the fighting, tragedies, pain and suffering in the world. We paint a dark perception of the world, designed to heighten fear and insecurity. This is good for selling drugs, alcohol, guns and ammunition, too, of course."

"Advertisements and the media also focus on desires for wealth, power, material things and sex. Much of the population has devoted their entire life's purpose to these things, which guarantees they will stay in the lower two or three chakras. Do you see how all of these things give the lower three chakras focus, and how all these motivations are focused on the individual and self-serving?"

"Now this makes a lot of sense," I said. "I think I am finally getting it."

"Yes," he agreed. "And all of these things also feed the animalistic ego instead of the soul. This is how we keep the masses in their ego. People in lower levels of consciousness will struggle with relationships, with their self-esteem, with money, with everything in their lives. Sex and money will be the primary goal of relationships. It will be extremely difficult for them to even question the paradigm of their slavery, let alone rise above it. And again, when they feel bad, there are plenty of drugs, alcohol and objects of desire to temporarily help them feel better."

"This is all such genius!" I applauded enthusiastically as I threw up my hands, then brought them back behind my head. I leaned back while beaming a radiant smile. I flashed back to the helicopter flight with Father, when he asked me why all the people were sitting in traffic on their way to work instead of enjoying the beautiful day at the beach. Then I laughed out loud at the beauty of it all. "Stupid slaves," I said to my teacher in pure joy.

He studied me for a few moments, then asked, "Is it OK if we walk and continue the lesson? We are not meant to sit all day long." It was a beautiful day, so I agreed quickly. He continued teaching as we walked for quite some time. Eventually, we got to a point in the middle of one of the huge lawns. Then he stopped and asked me, "How well do you know your mother?"

For some reason, I knew that we had just departed from the prescribed curriculum. "Not very well," I answered. "I usually get to spend a little time with her just one to three days per year."

It seemed as though he already knew this. He said, "Remember the part of today's lesson where I discussed different levels of consciousness, or energy?"

"Yes," I nodded in agreement, wondering where he would go next.

"Well," he said as he paused to consider what he was saying. "Your father and mother, they are like fire and water. They do not mix well. This is why the two are always apart."

"I've always wondered about that," I confessed. "But I'm sure every child wants their parents to be together."

"Yes," he agreed. "But that is not why I am telling you this." I knew he saw my surprise, so I waited for him to continue. He explained, "It's about you. One parent is fire. One is water. And you… you are like one of the two."

I later understood that while I thought I had understood what he meant at the time, I had barely scratched the surface as to the depth and ramifications of these differences. Perhaps if he had used the example of fire and gunpowder instead of fire and water, that would have been a more accurate comparison. Through all the time I studied with him, this was never brought up again. It seemed, by telling me this, that he had fulfilled some sort of obligation he had felt he needed to fulfill.

For the next two years, I studied the keys to the kingdom and many other lessons. I began meditating to quiet my busy mind, though my busy schedule did not always allow for it. These lessons opened up an entirely new world for me, and it was obvious why we kept such knowledge from the slaves. I learned examples of how great men had become great by advancing their level of consciousness. The level of work and accomplishment they achieved was in line with their level of consciousness. I learned that there was no end to knowledge, and that my curiosity would never be satiated. The simple question from that first day, "What do you think you are?" had such profound implications. I had never considered being more than the animal-type characteristics of flesh and bone.

Before I knew it, my sixteenth birthday arrived. That morning I was told Father would arrive for an early dinner at the house, and that he had a special gift for me. I never got gifts, so this was both incredibly stressful and exciting. The anticipation was killing me. The lessons crawled at a snail's pace that day. I got a chance to relax for an hour before the early dinner at five. I still rarely ever saw Father. I wasn't sure how dinner would go, but I was excited about the gift.

The chef set us up on the patio outdoors as the sun slowly sank toward the ocean, lighting up the clouds in magnificently bright yellow, blue and purple hues. The chef pulled out all the stops, starting with three different hors d'oeuvres, then medium-rare filet mignon and my favorite garlic mashed potatoes, plus a side of asparagus in an amazing sauce.

Father actually seemed in a decent mood. The rare times I had spent with him, he usually seemed preoccupied with other things. He asked me various questions on how I was doing, what I had been studying, what I had learned and even what I thought about some of the different aspects of the studies, especially the keys to the kingdom. There were a couple of things that he gave me some more advanced insights into, which impressed me. I realized I had learned much, but I had so much more to learn to even approach Father's knowledge. He'd been studying for fifty-three years.

As we were talking during the filet mignon main course, he surprised me. I'll never forget it. I was totally floored. He said, "Nigel, you have worked hard and learned much. While other kids have grown up playing, you have had lessons to learn every day. I am proud of you and your efforts." I inadvertently gulped when I heard his words and a chunk of beef dropped into my throat. Not only was I in utter shock, now I couldn't breathe. I tried to say something, anything. I couldn't.

"Do you have something to say?" he asked.

"Hell, yes – I'm freaking choking, you moron!" is what I tried to scream out, but nothing came out. I tried to swallow it. It wouldn't move. I tried to hawk it up and breathe it out. Nothing happened. I started feeling light-headed as panic seized my heart. I grabbed my throat with my left hand and shoved my right hand as deep as I could, trying to get my fingers down into my throat to get the filet mignon out. I started to black out. Then I felt grabbed from behind and lifted up as a fist was pulled strongly into my stomach, then again, then again, and one more time as the chunk of beef shot across the table. I gasped desperately for air – and the vitality of life began its return. I was lowered gently into my chair as I gulped in oxygen. Slowly my vision returned, and Father was staring at me eye-to-eye.

"Whew!" he exclaimed. "Looks like you're going to make it. Are you OK? How do you feel?" he asked.

"Give me a minute," I said hoarsely. I was totally embarrassed and nodded my head up and down as I coughed for a minute. Finally, I settled down and was able to drink some refreshingly cool water. "Sorry about that," I said.

Father chuckled a little and said, "Well, that was exciting. It would have been a hell of a way to go out on your sixteenth birthday, and such a shame with what awaits you later tonight."

"What is it?" I asked, as the curiosity drove me bonkers.

"It's a surprise, but you will like it. I promise," said Father with a strange smile that I had never seen before.

"Hmmmm. OK," I replied suspiciously. The entire experience was incredibly strange and foreign. Father almost seemed human. Something was definitely wrong. I felt better right away, and I made sure to triple-chew the rest of the beef and asparagus. Then dessert arrived. The chef was a master. He loved the chance to show off his culinary blessings. To top off the heavenly meal, he had baked a perfect souffle, which he paired with a homemade vanilla bean gelato.

Father was never much of a conversationalist, at least around me. Of all the people I had ever been around, he was by far the quietest. As the last few bites of dessert disappeared, Father asked me an interesting question, "From all that you have studied and learned so far, what creature do you think is the most dangerous?"

The answer seemed obvious to me, but I knew that answers to Father's questions were never obvious. "Humans are destroying the planet and have the power to kill and destroy unlike no other," I replied.

Father nodded patiently and then asked, "Can you be more specific? Which humans are the most dangerous in the world?"

Now that was a question that I really had to dig deep to find answers to. I looked at him as I begged inside for the right answer to come. And then I said, "Men like you."

Father burst into hysterical laughter, unlike anything I had ever seen before. He nearly fell off of his chair as he folded over, the convulsions shaking him uncontrollably while tears leaked out of his clenched eyelids. The laugh was contagious. I could not help but laugh at him laughing. I was serious with my answer and had not expected him to find it funny. I noticed the chef peek around the corner to witness the once-in-a-lifetime spectacle, which continued for a full two minutes before Father began to regain himself.

"That!" he finally was able to utter as the laughter slowed down. "That was the funniest thing I have ever heard." He wiped the tears from his face and dried his eyes with his white linen napkin. "Your answer is perfect, and absolutely true in many ways, which is why it struck me as so funny. However, it is not the answer I was looking for." He laughed out loud again, then said, "Sometimes, the teacher becomes the student. OK, so other than men like myself, who are the most dangerous human beings in the world?" he asked again.

"I come up with the best answer and, of course, it's not the one he was looking for," I thought with chagrin as I racked my brains once again. I thought about what I saw on the news. I thought about the poorest areas of the poorest countries I had traveled to, and all those people living in such terrible and sometimes even disgusting conditions. "But who is the most dangerous?" I asked myself again.

My thoughts wandered to the animal kingdom, where there were poisonous creatures and predators that could kill a man. I thought about how fiercely a mother bear and other animals would fight to protect their young. I tried to find correlations in human behavior. I said to Father, "Other than desperate people, I cannot think of anything else, Father."

Father nodded, "That is not a bad answer," he said. "Come," he got up and gestured for me to follow him inside. Our footsteps echoed through the vast rooms and hallways as I followed him to a now familiar place: the hall of kings.

Father turned to me and said, "In some ways, it was not a fair question for you, but you understand that life is not fair, yes?"

"Yes," I acknowledged.

He continued, "This human creature you have only studied from afar, but I assure you, it is the most dangerous, most ruthless, most cunning and most deceiving creature in all the world with no close second. Even I am not a close second to this deadly creature." He paused as he looked me in the eyes. "Have you found the answer?" he asked one more time.

I shook my head and admitted in defeat, "No, Father."

Father's gaze had not yielded when he said plainly, "A woman, is the answer." He waited in silence for me to grasp what he was saying before adding, "A woman is the most dangerous creature in the world. There is no close second." More silence followed as I pondered what he was saying. I struggled to grasp how a woman was the most deadly creature in all the world.

Then Father waved his hands upward and stretched his palms out as he said, "All of these great men, and all of their kingdoms, could have easily been destroyed by one single woman. A woman can get under your skin and directly poison your heart, such that there is nothing you would not do for her. Men have started wars because of women. Men have killed themselves and each other for women. Kingdoms have fallen in the name of love, simply because of a woman. They lure you in with a seemingly harmless smile, a laugh, their sweet perfumes, soft skin and sexual desire. Your heart surrenders to them, and then they own you." Father paused one last time for full effect, then he raised his voice and these words vibrated strongly down the massive hallway, "Make no mistake, my son, a woman is the deadliest of them all."

Then he relaxed ever so slightly and asked, "Do you understand what I am trying to tell you?"

I nodded and said, "Yes, Father."

"I want you to say it out loud," he added and repeated, "A woman is the deadliest creature in the world."

"A woman is the deadliest creature in the world," I repeated firmly.

"Very good," Father replied, seeming somewhat satisfied. I could see that his mind switched gears as his demeanor relaxed quite a bit. In a much more normal voice, he said, "As I said earlier, you have worked and studied hard. You have become a young man. Now you will begin to study this most dangerous creature. You like women, yes?" he asked.

One little question and my stomach splashed onto the stone floor as I reeled in awkwardness. "Yes," I admitted weakly. I was sure he was spying on my internet activity.

"OK. Good," he replied. "Remember in your studies of the entertainment industry and media. Women are taught to desire the rich prince. Well, my son, luckily for you, you are that rich prince. You are a king, just as I am, and all these great men in this hall. Women will throw themselves at you simply because of your money. And you've got my good looks," he added proudly. "So do not attach your feelings to any of them. They are a dime a dozen. Do you understand what I am saying?" he asked to reinforce the lesson.

"Yes. I understand, Father," I replied.

"Excellent," he said. "So, my birthday gift to you is to introduce you to your first lessons in women. You will experience how strong their lure can be over you, and you will begin to understand how strong your appeal to them is. I am giving you a full week off. Just pack some light, casual clothes for a week and grab your toothbrush and things. Do not bring your phone or laptop or anything for entertainment. You will not need them. Meet me at the front door in thirty minutes."

"Yes, Father," I answered with a half-smile. My mind was exploding with what he could have been talking about. "A week off?" That was a first. "Starting to study women…" I thought to myself. The concept certainly had my attention. I walked swiftly, straight to my room, which took a full minute. I grabbed my suitcase and threw it on the bed. I looked at all my casual shorts, t-shirts and other shirts and debated what to bring. I had no idea what to expect as I grabbed clothes, threw them in the suitcase, then changed my mind and switched them out. In what seemed like five minutes, it was twenty-five minutes later. I freaked out when I saw I was nearly out of time. Being late was never acceptable, and I wasn't about to miss this, whatever it was. I quickly grabbed some clothes, my toothbrush, toothpaste and deodorant, tossed them into the suitcase and zipped it up. Its wheels whirled loudly down the halls as I hustled toward the front door.

When I arrived to the reception area, Father was there with our driver and a security guard. "There's the birthday boy," Father announced, and he and the other two men smiled smiles that I had never seen before.

They were up to something, and the something was me. "This is either going to be the worst experience and scar me for life, or it's going to be really, really good," I thought.

"I won't be here when you get back in a week," Father said plainly. He turned and looked to the other two men and nodded, then the security guard opened the door as the driver grabbed my bag. It was pretty quiet in the car as we headed down the Pacific Coast Highway towards Los Angeles. I was lightly sweating, filled with anxiety of what this was all about as time slowed to a crawl. I guessed we would head for the airport, but to my surprise we headed toward downtown. Soon we were among the tallest buildings in the city.

The black Mercedes rolled up to the front of what looked like a really nice hotel. The driver parked in front, then got out and opened my door and then the trunk. He walked my suitcase through the glass double door, held open by two bellmen. The driver gave the bag to a bellman and then left, as the security guard and bellman escorted me to the elevator. I had been in a lot of nice hotels around the world. None were more elegant than this one, with its fine stone and mahogany. It was almost as nice as home. Inside the elevator, the security guard inserted a special key and the top penthouse button illuminated on the panel. "Oh yeah," I thought, trying unsuccessfully to hide my smile.

My feet pressed heavily into the floor as the elevator glided smoothly up, up, up, and up some more. Soon we were at the penthouse floor and the elevator doors slid open. The security guard turned to the bellman and said, "I'll take it from here." He took the suitcase and handed him a hundred-dollar-bill. I stepped into the reception room, which was beautifully done with dark, hand-carved mahogany walls and colorful paintings. We went through the door into the penthouse suite. It was very modern and elegant, but my attention immediately went elsewhere.

Standing in a line, shoulder to shoulder, stood six incredibly beautiful women. Each one of them was wearing only lingerie. I was absolutely speechless as I looked at them. They each smiled and waved to me. Stunned, I had no idea what was happening as I turned and looked at the security guard.

He chuckled in amusement. I cannot imagine the look on my face, but I'm sure it was priceless. He pointed to the distant kitchen. "In the kitchen on the island is the room-service menu, as well as menus from several of the finest restaurants nearby. I or another security guard will order all your food and anything else you require. We will wait outside by the elevator. There's no other way in or out. Just open the door and tell me what you want or slide a paper under the door. There are plenty of drinks and snacks in the kitchen." I looked at him blankly. I had no idea what he had just said. My mind was mush. I was just a little more interested in the women in lingerie. I think he figured this out.

He gestured to the women, and one by one, each one flashed a smile, said "Hi" and told me her name, and then twirled slowly around so I could see her thonged ass and flowing hair. I was trying not to be embarrassed as the untamed monster throbbed wildly in my shorts. The six women were: Caucasian blonde, Caucasian brunette, Caucasian redhead, Indian, African-American and Asian. It was like Baskin Robbins with vanilla, chocolate chip, strawberry, chocolate, dark chocolate and mandarin-orange sherbet.

The security guard looked me in the eyes and explained slowly, "If you like one, or two of them, simply pick them out. They will spend this week with you."

I must have looked like a deer in headlights as I looked at him, turned and looked at the women's beautiful bodies and smiling faces, then turned back to him. My adrenaline-ignited heart was banging like a bass drum through my entire body.

He looked at me with a gentle smile and asked, "Do you like any of them?" I nodded affirmatively. "Good," he replied as his smile widened. "Which one is your favorite?" he asked.

I turned and looked at the women again. They all looked incredible. The brunette, in particular, there was just something extra special about her. She was one of the most beautiful women I had ever seen. I cuffed my left hand over my mouth, trying not to offend anyone, as I whispered to him, "The brunette."

"OK. Good," he replied. "Do you have one more favorite?" he asked.

I cuffed my hand and whispered again, "The Asian."

"Excellent!" he exclaimed. He pointed to the brunette and Asian and said, "OK. You and you can stay." The two women looked at each other and grinned devilishly, then back at me. The security guard then said, "Thank you to the rest of you. You can get dressed and I'll let you out." As the four women waved and walked away, the beautiful brunette and Asian women smiled and walked up to me. I was still absolutely stunned and speechless.

The security guard chuckled and said, "You girls know what to do. Teach him well." I could not believe what was happening as the brunette took my right hand and the Asian woman took my left as they led me forward. Walking gingerly, I stared at the brunette's ass swaying side to side, then the Asian's ass, then back to the brunette's as they escorted me into the master bedroom and closed the door.

Now two pros on one rookie hardly seemed fair, but I wasn't complaining. I studied hard and they taught me well.

There were so many ways to give and receive. I'll never forget my first lessons at age sixteen, when I experienced how good it could feel to be a king.

CHAPTER 4

After my sixteenth birthday, life took on a whole new meaning. Words cannot describe how invigorating it was to be able to have sex with incredibly beautiful women. I was becoming a man – and I was getting good at it. It was a powerful feeling that was hard to describe with mere words. I began to understand what Father meant about the power of women. I still studied the family business all of the time, except on Saturday evenings. Saturdays, a young woman of my choice would come over and join me for dinner, then spend the night with me. I was still very socially awkward. I always seemed to make them laugh with the odd things I would say. I simply had not been around or talked to very many people in my life, except for my teachers. At one point, I realized that maybe this was why Father was so quiet. I wondered if he had been raised the same way he was raising me. That would have explained some things.

Time whizzed by as I settled into this new routine. Occasionally, when Father was there, he began to share with me specific examples of his business dealings. He even had me listen to some phone calls he put on the speaker phone in his office. Father did not mess around. He told people what to do, and I never heard anyone ever question it.

One of the family lawyers began to come in regularly and teach me about various aspects of the legal structures of some of our businesses. He educated me on how the multiple layers of corporate entities hid our identity and shielded us from liability, thereby protecting our wealth. He also gave me great insight into the specifics of how Father was the puppet master for various politicians and industry leaders. Most of these so-called leaders sold their souls willingly.

Representatives of our companies were on the boards of other companies. The same was true of industry regulators. For example, it was common for a leader of one of the chemical companies to leave the firm and then go work for the FDA or other governmental regulatory agency. Even more common, for individuals we wanted to influence, our representatives would offer high-paying jobs to their children or other family members. "Greed is the grease that turns the wheels of government and industry," Father would say. From what I saw, it worked every single time.

My lessons continued non-stop until age seventeen and a half, then something else unexpected happened. It was a cold and rainy day outside. Father was home, so he and I were having a meal in the massive dining room. The rare times I spent time with him, we still only ever talked about business. Father wanted to make sure I would be able to take over if and when the moment arrived. However, that evening he surprised me when he said, "I want you to go to college."

"Really?" I asked, which was a mistake. It was an unspoken rule to never question him in such a way.

He frowned a little and raised his eyebrows as he reaffirmed with a strong, "Yes." I had never expected to go to college. Now, with this news, the debate raged in my head. I didn't see much that I could learn. I had studied my whole life. So sitting in class did not have any appeal. But on the other hand, I would potentially have a lot more freedom. The thought of more freedom was exhilarating, but I did not show it.

Father continued, "I've arranged for you to go to Harvard, starting in the fall. Everything has been arranged. You will study law with some of the best legal minds in the world. Some of our future politicians and industry leaders will come out of there."

"Oh, great. How exciting!" the sarcastic thoughts screamed inside my head. "Yes, Father," I said out loud. I saw how becoming a legal expert would be an added strength for running the family business. Getting to know future politicians wouldn't hurt either. "It's always about the business," I reminded myself sadly.

"Great," he replied matter-of-factly. School starts in August. You will be there two weeks before school begins. Like all discussions with Father, that was the end of it.

I soon realized, however, that I found it pleasant to have something to look forward to. Going to Harvard was going to be a big change. My entire life had been so structured, and frankly, controlled. This was going to be a totally new and different experience. I would have my own place to stay. The closer and closer it got to August, the more curious and excited I became. I started driving lessons right away. I was going to have a car at school.

In the beginning of July, a woman came to see me. Father had asked her to study the current fashions at Harvard and then pick out a wardrobe for me. She was also a skilled tailor, so she measured me and had five different suits custom-made to fit perfectly. An entire year's wardrobe was ordered for me all at once and sent to my luxury condo near campus.

My mental debate as to whether college would be a total waste of time or a good experience intensified as the date for my flight from Los Angeles to Boston arrived. Father was not there to see me off. One of the security guards and the driver took me to the airport. The guard stayed with me for the entire trip, making sure that I arrived safely to my destination. The condo building was set up like a hotel, where the downstairs entrance had a bellman and there were always one or two security guards visible.

My guard carried my bag inside and accompanied me up the elevator and to the door of my condo. He opened the door, then checked everything inside, bade me good luck and left. As I sat down on the leather sofa in the living room, I realized that for the first time in my life, I was truly on my own. No security guards other than in the lobby. No driver. No chef. No Father. Other than the maid, who was scheduled to clean every Monday morning while I was at class, I was on my own. "This IS different," I said to myself, and a smile spread across my face. For the first time in my life, I felt free.

I enjoyed walking around campus and seeing the other students. The nearby coffee shops and restaurants were always buzzing. Walking around without a security guard felt amazing. I was a stranger in a wonderful new and strange land, and I felt safe. The condo was so small compared to home, but it felt like mine. It felt good.

I soon learned that Father had arranged some friends for me. I was instructed to go to a nearby café for a casual introduction. I guess this shouldn't have been a big surprise, but two other guys had started school at the same time and were in the law program also. So there we were, three strangers looking at one another, and now good friends. The first guy's name was Elliot. He was tall and pale-skinned with reddish blonde hair. He was from the UK. It was obvious the waitress loved his accent.

My second friend went by Jack. He was of Chinese descent from an old Hong Kong family, so his real name was much more exotic. He was short and thin with a bright smile. His sense of humor proved quite lively. We found that much of our class schedule was the same. I just assumed they were from a similar type of family. Through all the time I knew them, we never talked about family, which was perfectly fine with me.

Compared to all my other worldly outings, Harvard was a totally different experience. All of these people were either terribly smart, wealthy, or both. We seemed far away from the slaves. The conversations were brilliant, often esoteric, and the jokes were fantastic. Another thing that I had not expected was that the women would be so appealing. Here I was among thousands of women, all my own age, and they were a far cry from the women I had spent my Saturday nights with. These women were smart, confident, educated and motivated. They were... stimulating, to say the least.

I was still incredibly socially awkward compared to all of the other students. Jack and Elliot got much amusement and entertainment from me, and they teased me all the time. Somehow, though, these two really did seem like friends. I had never had friends before. I wondered what having brothers and sisters would have been like. Sometimes we even studied together, since we had the same classes. We could quiz and role play each other, and we were all doing well in school.

When we weren't in class or studying, we were chasing women. Jack and Elliot seemed at ease with the girls, and each of them soon had a girlfriend. Elliot had two, actually, until one found out about the other. November arrived, and I was still single and quite frustrated. That late evening we went for pizza at a little Italian place nearby. It was family-owned and known for its authentic cuisine. As soon as I walked in, I saw her. She smiled and waved us over and said, "Pick any table you want."

Her hair was long, thick, straight and black. Her skin was perfectly tan, and her smile was radiant beneath those dark-brown eyes. She was average height, maybe five foot four or five. I can't describe what it was about her. Obviously she was attractive, but I saw many attractive women every single day. I was totally distracted in her presence, and Jack immediately noticed. "How you doin'?" he said to me in a funny, rapper-style pick-up-line voice. He and Elliot both laughed out loud. I ignored them as I stared at her far away in the kitchen.

She brought us menus as we each ordered sodas. We debated like lawyers until we decided on an extra-large pizza with half pepperoni and sausage, half pepperoni and jalapenos. She took our order, smiled at me and then floated away like a goddess.

"Oh my God!" squeaked Elliot with excitement as she floated away. "I thought you were going to die an old lonely one-handed pervert, but I think she actually likes you," he teased and laughed out loud as Jack joined in. I laughed a little, too.

"She does like you," Jack agreed.

"She is fabulous," I muttered.

"You gotta go for it," Elliot prodded.

"It's hard to see myself dating a waitress," I confided. Each of them understood where I was coming from. If it was found out, it would be totally frowned upon. I would rather have been tortured and killed than have Father find out I was dating a waitress at a pizza place.

Jack quickly retorted, "Man, you're not marrying this girl. It's all just for fun. She would be a lot of fun. None of us are going to say anything." The three of us turned and stared at her taking an order a couple tables away.

"Jesus," was all I could say in both absolute lust and frustration.

"You are healed, brother!" Elliot announced, and we all laughed out loud again.

They continued to prod me as we slowly devoured the fantastic giant pizza. "These jalapenos are legit!" I said with delight.

"Fire in the hole!" said Jack, and we all laughed at the future ramifications.

Soon dinner was done and the suspense was intense. The pressure I had on myself was plenty, and that was multiplied tenfold by Jack and Elliot's expectations for me to do something. She asked if we wanted refills in to-go cups and then hooked us up. Then she brought us the check, looked at me and asked, "Can I get you guys anything else?"

I was absolutely spellbound. "Can I get your number?" I asked bravely.

"My number?" she asked with a bit of an attitude. "Why would I give you my number? I don't even know you."

"Well this is your chance to know me better," I replied. "And I can help you out."

"Help me out?" she asked, raising the pitch of her voice and verifying that is what I said. "With what?"

"You know," I explained, "With being a waitress and everything." Then, in what I experienced as a slow-motion video, I watched her reach her hand down to the table, grab my extra-large soda, lift it up and slowly pour it over my head. The ice-cold soda sent frozen lightning through me as it soaked my head and face, then rushed down the center of my back, all over my chest and lap. My mouth opened wide in pure shock, as I was totally stunned. Elliot and Jack immediately doubled over in laughter, crying because they were laughing so hard as the goddess stormed away.

"Oh my God!" Elliot squeezed out in utter delight between stomach-cramping laughs. "That was so awesome!" he squeaked in utter ecstasy. Jack was unable to speak, but he reached out and they gave each other high fives.

I threw some cash on the table and said, "Let's go," as I got up and walked out. They quickly followed me. Unfortunately, I had driven us all to the restaurant. Elliot and

Jack laughed and teased me the entire way home. I was in shock. I had no idea why she had poured my soda all over me. Obviously, she was upset. As I parked near Elliot's place, I said, "Guys, seriously, why did she get so upset?"

"She's obviously got some issues," said Elliot in a supportive tone.

Jack shared something more insightful. "You told her she needed help," he explained, "Because she was a waitress. She saw that you were judging her as being inferior or needy."

"I was judging her as being inferior or needy?" I repeated out loud. I didn't get it.

"Yes," Jack answered. "What did you mean when you said you could help her out?"

I explained, "Well, she's a waitress, so obviously, she doesn't have or make a lot of money, so I was offering to help her out with some money."

"This may come as a surprise to you," Jack replied. "But not everyone cares about money. She may have felt like you were offering her money to date you, almost like you were offering to buy her, like she was a prostitute. Some guys with money treat women like this all the time, so it's possible guys have literally offered her money for sex before. She's beautiful."

"So, she felt like I was treating her like a prostitute?" I asked in surprise.

"Basically, yes," he answered.

"Whoops!" I exclaimed humorously and Jack and Elliot both laughed out loud.

"It's a shame, man," Elliot said. "That pizza was to die for. I don't know if I can show my face in there again and get out alive."

He and Jack laughed out loud one more time as Jack agreed and said, "You know it!"

"It's OK," Elliot confided as he and Jack got out of the car. "There are plenty of fish in the sea."

We said goodbye and my mind flooded with self-doubt and regret all the way home. Over and over I replayed the video in slow motion while asking questions. "Did I treat her like a prostitute because I'm used to being with prostitutes? Are there really women who don't care about money?" I thought about what Father had said on my sixteenth birthday, how women throw themselves at the prince. "Maybe Elliot and Father are right. Women are a dime a dozen. There are plenty of fish in the sea." But I couldn't get her out of my mind. I felt bad that I may have hurt her in some way.

Thanksgiving arrived, and everyone traveled to spend time with their families. Everyone except me, that is. I spent the four-day weekend alone and caught up on my studies. Semester final exams were a few weeks later, followed by Christmas and New Year's. Both Jack and Elliot left during the school breaks, so I was alone. This was by far the hardest time in my life at that point. I'd never had much fun growing up, but at least I had a purpose and a home, and there were always other people around to take care of me. I realized that I wasn't very good at taking care of myself. I had gained twelve pounds in the first semester, overeating and drinking soda. I felt as though I didn't fit in with most of the other students. I felt like a failure not having a girlfriend. And the waitress nightmare haunted me incessantly. I still couldn't get her out of my mind.

Then one cold Sunday evening in early January, I got super pissed off at myself and made a decision. I was going to go back to the Italian restaurant and explain myself to the waitress. I expected to get another ice-cold soda poured over my head, but I was tired of feeling like a total loser and not doing anything about it. "Kings do not wallow in self-doubt and pity," I told myself. I thought of the hall of kings and Father. "I am better than this," I thought encouragingly.

When I arrived near the restaurant, I drove by it slowly, trying to see through the windows if she was there. Then I drove by from the other direction. I couldn't tell. There were no cars in the parking lot, so the restaurant looked dead. "Grow some balls," I chided myself, so the next time around I parked. A young couple exited the restaurant, then passed me as I went inside. Sure enough, there she was. I had entered while she was clearing a table with her back to me. She turned and quickly yelled, "Just a min…" She stopped abruptly right there, immediately recognizing me. "What are you doing here?" she asked, with a sharp edge to her voice.

"I came to see you," I answered. I may have looked calm on the outside, but my insides were like a rollercoaster screaming down from its peak.

"You've got some nerve," she replied coldly, as she folded her arms across her chest.

I took some steps to halve the distance between us. "That night. It's haunted me ever since. I wanted to tell you I'm sorry," I said. Once I uttered those words, it was as if a lightning bolt had struck me. I realized that this was the first time I had ever apologized to anyone. I realized I was just like Father. I felt horrible.

"Really?" she said, in a disbelieving tone, with her eyebrows raised.

"Yes," I replied. I took a few more steps toward her while she stood her ground in silence.

"I'm sorry," I said. Fireworks exploded throughout my body as the tension of the moment collided with the amazing feelings of seeing her again.

Her stare was intensely burning through me. After a long silence, she asked, "What are you sorry for?"

I nodded, then explained, "I'm sorry for judging you, for thinking you needed help." I looked at her. She studied me for what seemed like eternity.

"Hungry?" she asked as her arms unfolded and relaxed.

"Sure!" I lied.

"Have a seat," she said as she pointed to the nearest booth. The restaurant was completely empty.

"Do you know what you want?" she asked.

"I know what I came here for," I answered confidently.

"OK, what's that?" she asked curiously.

"Well, pepperoni jalapeno pizza, of course," I teased. She laughed.

"Coming right up," she said and then floated back to the kitchen.

She returned with two large sodas and sat down across from me. "Now I've got double-firepower," she teased, holding the sodas before handing me one of them.

"It's OK. I wore my swimsuit underneath my pants just in case," I advised. She laughed heartily.

"I did feel a little bad, like I overdid it," she confessed.

"It's OK," I added. "It'll make such a great story when we tell people how we first met." Her angelic smile beamed at that one. I was surprising myself. The nervousness was totally gone now. I was back in. I felt comfortable with her, like a belonging. I'd never felt anything like it before.

"So tell me about you," she said with a smile. I laughed uncomfortably at that. I realized that I had never told anyone about myself before.

"I'm a bit unusual," I confessed. "I've never told anyone about myself before."

"So mysterious," she teased.

I was more serious as I said, "I never went to school, until college. I never had pizza before, until college. I never had friends, until college, so I'm a bit socially awkward at times. Before college, I'd never told anyone my name was Nigel. I don't have a family that does things or spends holidays together. Before now, I'd never apologized to anyone. I'm a bit unusual, but I am learning."

"Wow," she said as she contemplated everything I had said. "You ARE really weird!" she teased. "What did you do before college?" she inquired.

"I studied. I have had teachers and lessons from a very early age, as long as I can remember," I replied.

"What did you study?" she asked.

"Life. Animals. How the world works. Business. People," I answered.

"What did you do for fun growing up?" she asked.

"Nothing," I said.

"No sports? No hobbies?" she asked.

"No," I remarked plainly.

"You haven't lived!" she exclaimed.

"I learned at an early age that sports and hobbies were not a priority over my lessons," I explained.

"That's terrible," she said. "Do you have any favorite vacations? Or travel anywhere?"

I replied, "For some of my studies, I did get to travel. I did enjoy that. I've been to a handful of countries in Europe, a few in Asia, Mexico, Canada, Hawaii. Tell me about you," I prodded.

She lit up as she started talking. "I have fond memories of my family growing up. My father owns this place, so I started helping out here when I was young, but not a lot until I was older. Most of our vacations were to beaches. I love to play in the water, surf, boogieboard, snorkel, you name it. I would love to scuba dive or learn to sail someday. In the winter, I love to snowboard. There's nothing quite like being up on the mountain. It's so peaceful and stunning. Hiking and being outdoors gives me such joy. I feel so blessed in this life."

"Wow!" I remarked. "You light up when you talk about these things. I can see the passion and joy on your face. You are so beautiful," I said.

"Oh, thank you!" she said sweetly while beaming. She looked back at the kitchen and then said, "Looks like it's dinner time. I'll be right back." I watched her float back to the kitchen, and then float back with a nice hot pizza. One half had pepperoni and jalapenos. The other half had pepperoni, mushrooms, black olives and feta.

"Thank you. This is fabulous," I said with a smile.

"You're welcome," she replied happily.

We enjoyed the pizza and conversation. I'm not sure why, but it really did seem like she liked me. She actually finished her half before me, which was impressive. As I polished off the last bite, I said, "That was perfect."

"What, no dessert?" she asked.

"You want dessert?" I replied.

"You gotta get the girl dessert on your first date," she teased.

I laughed. "I didn't realize this was a date," I said. "I'm not exactly a dating expert," I confessed.

"Really?" she teased sarcastically, and we both laughed. I was in heaven, and it seemed like she was there right next to me. She floated back to the kitchen, and in a few minutes returned with a gift from the gods. It was a very small pizza pan, maybe eight inches in diameter, with a partially baked chocolate chip cookie on the bottom, covered with three large scoops of vanilla ice cream. I had never had such a delicious dessert before. We each had a spoon and ate from the same dish, which was also fun.

At the end of dessert, I said with a huge smile, "I've had an amazing time tonight. Thank you."

"It's been amazing for me, too," she said with her radiant smile.

"When can I spend more time with you?" I asked.

"I'm off on Thursday night," she answered. Then she gave me her number.

"Perfect," I said. I reached into my pocket and put some cash on the table to pay for dinner.

"No. No," she said. "Your money's no good here," she explained with a smile.

I wasn't about to try and offer her money again. "Thank you," I replied warmly. When I got up to leave, she got up, too, and then gave me a hug. Another lightning bolt zapped every essence of my being. That was my first genuine hug from anyone other than my mother as a little boy. Something so simple as a hug, I could not believe how good it felt. I would have stood there forever.

When she pulled away, our eyes met briefly before she turned away and said, "I'll see you Thursday. Can you pick me up here at six o'clock?"

"Yes," I answered with my own beaming smile. Then we parted ways and I floated out to the car. I was giddy as I glided out of the parking lot.

"Yes! Yes! Yeeeeesssssssss!" I yelled triumphantly as I banged on the steering wheel after getting far enough down the road where I wouldn't be heard. "She is incredible!" I exclaimed as I replayed the entire evening.

And that, my friends, is how Jessica and I met and started dating. Over the next four months she taught me how to live. She took me to the mountains to play in the snow. She took me to the beach. She took me surfing. She accepted me and all my weirdness. She always gave and never took. She taught me how to snuggle. She taught me how to love. Above all, she showed me the incredible person that I could be for someone.

Like a flash, the spring semester came to an end. Father had made arrangements for me to go back to the Los Angeles estate for the summer. I had been dreading this moment ever since early January. I picked up the phone to call him. Until this phone call, I had not talked to Father the entire school year. He liked the directness and brevity of texting. "I want to stay here for the summer," I said. "I'll take summer classes to get ahead."

"No. That's ridiculous. You need to come home," he said.

I braced myself and said, "Father, I'm dating someone. I want to stay here for the summer. I'll take summer classes."

"You're dating someone?" he asked.

"Yes," I admitted. "I met her at school," I lied.

"What's her name," he asked.

"Jessica," I responded.

"You remember the important lessons about women, yes?" Father asked.

"Yes, Father," I replied.

"How long have you been dating?" he asked.

"Just a couple months," I lied.

"You must get rid of her at three months, six months at the very latest. Do not get attached. You are not marriage material. Do you understand?" he asked firmly.

"Yes, Father," I replied. I had no intentions of getting rid of Jessica. I was so in love it was ridiculous. I could see now what Father meant when he said that women were the most dangerous creatures on Earth. There's nothing I wouldn't do for her. Little did I know how much that was going to be tested.

"I see you've been traveling around a little bit, too," he said. I know Father regularly looked at my credit card statements, but this was the first time he had ever commented about it. "What have you been doing?" he asked.

"I've just explored a few different activities. I'm learning," I explained. I'm sure he knew my answer was total bullshit and I cringed while I waited for his response.

"If your grades falter whatsoever, your days at Harvard are over," he said firmly. "You're young and still naive in some things. Don't screw this up. Do you understand?" he asked.

"Yes, Father," I answered. This was followed by a lengthy silence as my mind scrambled through all the possible things he might be thinking and say next.

"You can stay for the summer," he said as absolute joy exploded from my soul. "Take a full summer course load. Don't make me regret this."

"Yes, Father," I answered, trying to speak plainly and hide my exuberance. Then he hung up.

"Yes!" I yelled as loud as I could and immediately texted Jessica the good news. I had picked up a second cell phone to communicate with her, that I paid for with cash, so that it would be separate from Father's accounts. I didn't want any possibility of him spying on our communication or finding out all the details about her.

Honestly, after the all the grueling lessons I had growing up, Harvard was easy. The legal courses required a lot of time but were not complicated. After the phone call, I figured as long as I kept my straight A's, Father would give me some leeway into traveling and maybe even lighten up about my time with Jessica.

All or part of this conversation must have sounded some alarm that told Father he needed to keep a closer watch on me. Ever since that phone call, Father called me once per month. I became even more careful about my time and activities with Jessica, paying cash when we took little trips or went to dinner. She always paid for herself for everything.

When September arrived, I told Father that it hadn't worked out with Jessica, and I was now dating someone new named Alex, short for Alexandra. She was a friendly classmate of mine.

"Perfect," Father said. "Just don't get attached," he reminded me. "They have their evil ways."

I made sure I kept my grades up, and I continued the charade of changing dating partners, or even being single at some points. "School is just too intense right now, Father," I would say. "I don't have time for women." He liked that.

Jessica and I continued to date all this time. We fit together like two puzzle pieces. She helped me laugh through my childhood and family oddities. I could be myself with her. She was an angel. She was my everything.

When summer break arrived again, Father insisted I return to Los Angeles. I could not sway him this time. So Jessica and I did not communicate a single time during that two and a half months. I would not risk it. I knew how rigid Father was, and I had no idea how I was going to pull off being with Jessica after college.

Jack and Elliot understood my dilemma. They proved to truly be real friends. They did not say a word about Jessica and me to their respective families. We knew there had to be connections there.

When summer break finally ended, it was so incredible to be with Jessica again. They say that absence makes love grow fonder, and that was certainly the case for us. I wanted to just run away with her and never be found. I realized that was probably unrealistic, but I started to save cash. I would take two or three hundred dollars per week out of the ATM for so-called spending money. Instead of spending it, Jessica would bring pizza or we would eat at home or something cheap. I would also buy something with a credit card and then return it for cash or sell it on craigslist. Father would never miss these small amounts of cash.

Jessica and I were amazing together. It was effortless. I continued to spin the web of lies to Father as I continued to evolve. The little free time I had, I studied over and over what Father called the keys to the kingdom. He used them for his own selfish reasons. I remembered what the teacher had shared with me during our walk about Mother and Father, and I began to get greater insight into the power of the heart and the higher chakras. I began to realize what true power might be, and I formed new beliefs that contradicted some of Father's teachings. My intuition was growing stronger. I knew that Father and I were two freight trains barreling down the same track toward each other. One small love was going to face and fight all the power and money in the world. Two unbreakable forces were going to collide, and one or both would shatter.

CHAPTER 5

Time passed swiftly, and before I knew it, I graduated Harvard with perfect grades and honors. All the top law firms wanted me, but I was instructed to help Father with the family business. He told me to come back to the family estate in Los Angeles. I told him I would move back to Los Angeles, if required, but I wasn't going to live on the family estate any more.

"You don't understand who you are," he said strongly. "There are powerful forces in the world that will want to kidnap or kill you. There's a gentlemen's understanding that we don't mess with the kids while they are in school, but that is the only limitation."

"I don't care," I said. Wow, did that set off an explosion on the other end of the phone, which started with, "It's for your own good! Who do you think you are, standing up to me? Without me you are nothing! I could squash you in an instant!" On and on he went as I held the phone a full arm's length away from my ear.

"OK, OK," I said after the torrid lashing waned. "Listen, Father, for once. I've had a taste of freedom here. I cannot go back. But I will take your advice. I would love to have security guards watching my home. I am willing to live near the family estate, if I must. But honestly, you're almost never there, or if you are, you are busy, so what's the point? I could live anywhere." A long silence followed. At times, I could hear Father muttering his thoughts indiscernibly to himself.

"I will call you back," he said shortly. Then "Click!" he had hung up the phone.

"Wow!" I exclaimed out loud, followed by a gigantic exhale. The inevitable battle had begun with the smallest of skirmishes. "I suppose that was to some degree a success," I thought, but it was impossible to know yet. I certainly wasn't going to celebrate anything, knowing the impending collision.

"It'll be OK," said Jessica from behind, as she rubbed her hands down the back of my shoulders and back – then wrapped her arms around my torso. giving me a comforting hug. I put my hands on hers and just dissolved into her in the silence. Then without words, I turned around to face her, kissed her, caressed her, and we made love all afternoon.

Later, Father decided to relent on requiring me to move back to the family estate. I felt he didn't have much of a choice, though he could have cut me off financially so I wouldn't have been able to afford my own place or any security. But then I would have had to take a job with a law firm and work crazy hours for them, leaving little time for the family business.

He did require me to move back to Los Angeles, so I picked out a small home on top of a hill, with incredible views. It was a little over an hour from the family estate. Being on top of the hill made it easy for the security cameras and motion detectors to scan the area, so it was a good strategy for limiting the number of security personnel I had to have on site. I hired two guards so that I would always have at least one on site or to take me around. I paid them very well, plus an extra thousand dollars cash each week to stay quiet about Jessica. I also spoiled them with food and kindness to keep them loyal. Trust me, this was the best gig they would ever have.

I was also allowed to drive with a security guard as a passenger. The car was outfitted with bulletproof glass, and Kevlar plates were inserted into the door panels.

Jessica moved into a nearby apartment and easily got another job waiting tables. I admired her humility, and her smile was always present. I wondered if I could keep our secret long enough until Father passed away or somehow became incapacitated. I knew it was unlikely, but a guy could always dream, right?

It didn't take long for me to realize what I had gotten myself into. The demands of the family business were intense, and Father did not hesitate to throw me into the fire. He sent me to Hong Kong. The Hong Kong business was one of our strongest, riding the recent strong decades of growth in China. We exported chemicals and had a few other smaller businesses there.

There were a handful of very powerful Chinese families that had apparently united to oust what remained of the British Empire in Hong Kong. Well, that was us. Father's nickname there was "the White Tiger." In Hong Kong, the family estate was more like a fortress. If I dared go into the city, we traveled with multiple cars and a security team that literally surrounded me. If you've ever seen any of the American mafia movies, this would give you an understated idea of what was happening in Hong Kong. Asians were particularly ruthless, and at times they preferred knives over guns. It was bloody.

Occasionally, there would be a raid on one of our warehouses, but much more often, our delivery trucks just wouldn't make it to their destination. There was no negotiating with these other families at the moment. We were simply at war. My main role was to make sure that the layers of men below me stayed loyal, and that we hired the best mercenaries. Backpacks of cash flowed out of the family estate like milk from a dairy farm. This was a small expense compared to the volume of chemicals pumping out of our factories. But to keep the men loyal, you had to be present. This was a big problem. It would have been suicide to stay anywhere other than the family estate, so I couldn't have Jessica there. Being away from her was killing me. Three months passed swiftly, then six. I could see no end in sight.

Father called one late afternoon. He said, "I need you in India right away. The jet will be there to pick you up in three hours." Then, "Click." I sighed out loud as I rubbed both palms up and down my face. Then I notified security to set up an escort to the airport, and I packed my things. Thirty minutes later, six sleek black Mercedes limousines glided out of the estate gates, with me in the third car. Each car had five men in it, so I was in the middle of the back seat with a security guard on each side. The driver was playing classical music as I caught up on some business email on my phone while we cruised through the city.

Suddenly, the driver slammed on the brakes, launching all my weight forward while the seat belt pressed deeply into my hips and chest. A large industrial truck for hauling gravel had pulled out in front of the first Mercedes, which slammed on its brakes and skidded sideways, stopping just a few feet before the gravel truck, while the five trailing Mercedes slammed on their brakes trying to avoid one another. The sounds of two cars colliding behind me was more than alarming. That was just the warm-up.

Machine-gun fire erupted from all around us as the bullets pinged all over the car, denting the glass all around me. The glass went from clear to milky with each bullet's impact. The other cars did not have bullet-proof glass so their windows could roll down. The other five Mercedes' guards began returning fire. I was in the middle of a war zone, and the one goal of the war was to kill me. Since my car had bulletproof windows, they figured out pretty quickly which car I was in. The bullets sprayed onto the car faster than anything I could possibly describe. The sound was deafening and terrible. Then, it got even worse.

One motorcycle raced between the Mercedes limos, spraying machine gun fire from up close, catching our guards by surprise and killing several of them. Then a second zoomed in and screeched to a halt near my car. Through the thick, damaged, milky glass, I saw him pull the pins and then gently toss two grenades, underhand, beneath my car. Before I could say anything, the driver punched the accelerator as I sank back into the seat. We collided into the car ten feet in front of us, throwing me forward again. Our car pushed the other car forward another twenty feet as the grenades exploded behind us while bullets relentlessly pelted our car. I don't even know how the driver could see out of the windshield anymore. He then slammed the car into reverse and punched it, launching my weight forward again.

I couldn't see what we hit, but it felt as though one of the motorcycles was bounced off the rear of the car before we spun to the right and hit something much more solid, bringing us abruptly to a stop. Bullets rained onto the front of the car as it roared forward and swung to the left, veering onto the other side of the road and away from the ambush. Sparks flew from the dangling rear bumper as it dragged on the road behind us. I never saw the men from the other cars again, except for pictures of the blood-stained pieces of them that were delivered to the family estate the next day.

We made it to the airport without any further trouble. I'm sure pictures of our car were posted everywhere on social media that day. It's hard to describe how the car looked when the five of us got out to see it, thankful to be alive. We staggered out and stood there in awe as we looked around the Mercedes. Some of the bullets themselves were still on the car, smashed flat by the unyielding impact, filling the dent they had made. There were barely any spaces more than an inch apart between dents all around the car. "Looks like it's time to trade her in," I said, and everyone exploded in laughter, releasing all the pent-up stress of nearly dying.

My driver got a two-hundred-thousand-dollar bonus that night, and all the remaining guards got big bonuses, too. For the first time in my life, I was relieved to get on an airplane to go see Father. In India, little did I know, I was in for another surprise.

CHAPTER 6

The jet wasted no time taking off. As its engines roared, we accelerated down the runway and then lifted off the ground and soared into the darkness. All the twinkling lights of Hong Kong soon disappeared in the distance. A tall glass of scotch went down the hatch in seconds. "What the hell am I doing?" I asked myself, as my unrelenting thoughts held me prisoner. Then, I wondered what could have been so urgent in India.

The flight went smoothly. I passed out, crashing hard from the adrenaline rush of the ambush, followed by the scotch, until the jet's tires bouncing on the runway in India woke me. Eight cars were there waiting for me, far more than normal. The ride to the family estate was without incident. I was escorted into the home, then the head butler informed me that Father was expecting me in his study, and led me to meet him.

"Sounds like you had an exciting trip!" Father said with a chuckle. I didn't find it funny.

"They fricken' tried to kill me!" I yelled, feeling the reality of it.

"It's always scary the first time," he said, trying to comfort me. "The next times won't be so bad. You get used to it, just like everything else."

"I don't want to get used to it!" I said loudly.

"Calm down," he said firmly. I just stood there and looked at him.

"Sit," he said, like I was a finely trained pit bull, pointing to a nearby chair. I hesitated with my jaw clenched, then obliged.

"I'll get you some women for tonight," he said. "That'll get the stress out."

I shook my head and said, "I don't want any women."

This surprised him. He said, "Are you into guys now? I'm OK with that, I guess."

"No, Father," I replied. "I'm just not in the mood, in case you can't tell already."

"Nonsense," he said.

"Whatever," I replied. What had lately become the typical period of silence followed as we sat there looking at each other.

"Things were going relatively well in Hong Kong until this," he said. "The business is still growing and pumping out more cash than ever. We just need to survive in order to keep the men on board. There's more than enough money to fund an army there."

"Looks like we need one," I remarked, then went silent again.

Father looked me over for a while, then said, "What doesn't kill you makes you stronger, my son. With the right perspective, you can learn to see such experiences as positives that help you develop."

"Whatever," I replied coldly.

Father looked at me again for about ten seconds, then said, "Go get some rest. We'll talk more tomorrow." He pointed me toward the door. I gladly obliged.

I was beginning to understand much more about Father, how such a life can forge such a man. My early experiences with Jessica were enlightening. They made me realize that I was on the path to become my Father. Now, I had strayed far from that path, but I was living my Father's life still. I was miserable. The only thing that kept me going each day was the thought of being with Jessica again. I had not brought my extra cell phone with me, not expecting to be away for so long, and I wanted to protect us. I wondered how she was doing. I imagined her beautiful smile floating in and out of the restaurant near LA, and all our memories together. Clinging to the past, I slept poorly that night.

A welcome surprise came at breakfast, when Mother joined me. I got up to give her a hug, which surprised her. I had not seen her since before I went to college. During the few summer breaks I had spent in Los Angeles, it was simply too hot in India to visit. Sitting across the table, Mother had immediately sensed that something was different about me. She looked around to make sure no one else would overhear her. "You've changed," she said, as she examined me up and down.

Then I looked around before saying, "Yes. I have." She snuck a quick smile at me, and it was one of pure joy. I returned it, as tears welled up in my eyes before I shut them down. I didn't know what had come over me.

She leaned forward and whispered, "I can see your heart is open. You're in love."

"Holy shit!" I thought as my emotions went supernova inside. A tear slipped out of each of my eyes, giving me away. My deepest secret had been revealed in mere seconds to my Mother. Fear streaked through me that Father would find out. My heart pounded inside my chest as I gulped a big breath. Somehow, I knew she sensed my fear. She began to eat breakfast and I followed suit, as the head butler came over to check on us. We would talk normally or a little louder, exchanging the normal pleasantries about how school was and those types of things, but the whispers continued off and on between visits from the staff.

What the "keys to the kingdom" teacher had shared with me was being proven to me now. Only in an arranged marriage could two people so vastly different in levels of consciousness have been brought together. I understood why Father couldn't spend time with Mother, even though she was incredibly beautiful. They were polar opposite magnets, literally pushing them apart from one another.

"I'm happy for you," she whispered. "She must be amazing." I nodded thankfully. Then later, "What are you going to do?" she asked.

"I don't know," I confessed as I shrugged my shoulders. "But I have to do something," I whispered. We continued to enjoy breakfast, as I could tell she was pondering what to tell me next. We were nearly done when mother asked for another round of fresh mangos and other fruits, which sent the butler and staff back to the kitchen again.

"You must not force it," she whispered. "If it is meant to be, it will work out. That is the way of things. That is the way of love." That was all the insight she had to share with me. I wanted more. I wanted to know specifically what to do. Patience was my evil nemesis. It was torture. I was so miserable. People were trying to kill me, for crying out loud. A deep sigh exhaled out of me with the last bite of mango.

"Never give up," was her final whisper.

We got up from the table and came together and hugged sincerely, when Father appeared around the corner. He immediately stopped in his tracks. I felt his cold stare upon us. As Mother separated from me and walked out of the room, his cold stare targeted her like a laser beam until she disappeared from sight. I said nothing, waiting for Father to say something. He looked at me coldly, then walked past me and into the kitchen. I didn't hesitate to go back to my room.

"That was interesting," I thought as I replayed the conversation with Mother. "She is truly gifted. Such an awareness she has." Then I felt sorry for her, living the life she had. Married to someone so completely different, and spending her life alone in a cold, empty estate. Now that I knew what love was, my heart bled for Mother. Her father was a land baron in India. When Father married her, he received the rights to land the size of Arizona. Mother's father received the protections that came with being associated with Father's empire. It was a powerful merger.

"Maybe I can help her someday," I thought. Then I remembered her words, "You must not force it. Never give up." Then I thought, "Patience, I hate your guts." I had never been the religious type, but right then and there I dropped to my knees and prayed, as my heart overflowed from its burdens. My huge tears splattered like monsoon raindrops upon the cold, white marble tile. I had never cried like that before. I had never felt like that before.

Later, I went for a walk outside. This estate was basically a massive palace, built on a massive piece of land. Around the home were beautiful, carefully manicured gardens filled with flowers, fruit trees and ponds. I always found myself finishing the end of my walks at the tiger pen, which was a little behind the main house on the left side. The female tiger was lying lazily beneath the shade of the two trees in the back. I had always been captivated by the tiger's magnificence. Just like lions in Africa, they were kings of the jungle here, far above all other predators except man. And if a man had no weapons, he too would be easy prey for the tiger.

"I have something to show you," Mother's voice surprised me from behind. I smiled as I turned around. "You must keep it a secret. Quickly!" she whispered.

"OK!" I whispered with an agreeing nod.

Later that afternoon, Father and I were sitting on the large back patio, overlooking the back of the estate's gardens, acreage and beautiful mountains in the background. "What do you think we should do about Hong Kong?" he asked, as he watched for how I would respond. I sighed.

"Hire more mercenaries and give everyone raises," I said.

"What does that accomplish?" he asked.

"It keeps the staff loyal and our numbers up," I replied.

"That does nothing," he said coldly. After a long pause, he explained, "They will not work for you if they are certain they are going to die. There is only one way to deal with this." He paused to make sure he had my attention. "An eye for an eye. We will hit them back twice as hard. No one fucks with the White Tiger," he said, as he looked me defiantly in the eyes. He could see that I wasn't excited about the idea. He pounded his fist on the table so hard that his glass of water flew off and shattered upon the tile floor. "You are too soft!" he yelled, as he got in my face. "Twenty-two years old and you are still not a man! I will make a man out of you yet!" he promised.

The head butler appeared after hearing the glass shatter, and waved a servant over to clean up the mess. Father looked at him and said, "Tell Ahmad it is time." Ahmad was the estate's head of security. I had no idea what it was time for. Father looked at me sternly and said, "You WILL learn."

A servant brought Father a new glass of water as he and I sat there in the silence. I could feel his intensity boiling. A couple of minutes went by before some men appeared from around the left side of the house, back near the tiger pen. Ahmad and three other security guards were leading another man, who was blindfolded with a pale white strip of cloth tied around his head. Father looked at me and said strongly, "Come." He got up and walked toward the men as I followed him. As he approached, one of the security men opened the door to the tiger pen, while the others escorted the blindfolded man inside. They walked him in midway, where there was a metal pole sticking out of the ground. On the pole was a shackle, which they placed around the man's ankle and put a padlock on it. The man stood there, unaware of what awaited him, as Father walked up to the pen and grabbed the long whip that was hanging there.

As a security guard held the pen's door open for Father, Father gestured to me to follow him inside. I looked at the tiger, who was lying there attentively, watching every step we made. She began to growl and show her fangs as Father got closer. The blindfolded man heard the tiger and began to panic, jerking his leg uncontrollably, desperately trying to get out of the shackle. We walked up to a line three feet in front of the blindfolded man, where the grass had been cut away to leave a thick line in the dirt.

Father turned to me and said, "This man was caught stealing from the family business. Maybe as much as twenty-five or thirty thousand US dollars he stole from us."

The man heard him and pleaded loudly, "Please! I am sorry! My daughter was injured. The hospital bills and the medicine were too much. I will pay you back! I will do anything! Please let me go. Please!"

Father coldly looked me in the eyes, then he turned to the blindfolded man and said, "All who work for me know that I have no mercy. Whatever she leaves of you, THAT can go free." Then Father unwound his whip and snapped it toward the tiger, who got on her feet quickly and roared a frightening roar. The blindfolded man was now frozen like a statue in fear, quivering. Father pointed to the line to remind me to stay on the far side of it, then he snapped his whip at the tiger once more.

She bolted toward him as he stepped in back of the line. I was awestruck by her quickness. She flew like lightning, faster than my eyes could follow, and she roared like thunder that struck deep in my soul. The chain holding her whooshed as it unfurled. As she lunged toward Father with her fangs ready to crush him, the chain snapped tight at its full length, immediately stopping her ferocious attack. Claws outstretched, she turned and lashed at the blindfolded man, who screamed the most terrible of screams. I turned my head and closed my eyes. I could watch no more, but I could not escape the sounds that still haunt me in my sleep.

Father turned to me and said loud enough for all to hear, "THIS is the fate for those who betray me. Do not forget it." Then he walked swiftly toward the pen's door, which swung open for him, and he handed Ahmad the whip to rehang. I followed right behind him, distancing myself from the horrifying sounds behind me. I looked up as I walked out. Mother was watching everything from her upstairs balcony. After I saw her, she turned and went inside.

When we got inside the house, Father turned to me and said, "We leave at six AM for Hong Kong. Make sure you have a good suit on, and are packed and ready to go."

"Yes, Father," I replied, as he had already turned and started to walk away. "God, that was terrible," I thought to myself. "So absolutely, horribly terrible." I wanted to throw up but I refused to show my weakness as I turned and headed for my room. I skipped dinner, packed my things and waited for morning to arrive. "I can't wait for Hong Kong," I thought sarcastically. I liked business in America far better, where we pulled the strings for others to do the dirty work. But in Asia, Father took pleasure in doing it himself.

I slept on and off that night, haunted by the earlier horrific sights and sounds. It was all surreal. Life had deviated so far from the casual days of college and love. I was in the trenches of a bloody war now, a war among kings obsessed with power and money. I was up at five AM sharp, shaved, showered, suited and in the reception area at ten minutes before six. Father arrived shortly, and the security entourage escorted us safely to the airport and onto the jet. The flight was a little awkward, but I didn't care. Father and I didn't speak, except about trivial matters, for the entire journey. We were both preoccupied with what was to happen in Hong Kong. Thoughts of Jessica floated in and out of my mind. Our love seemed like only a distant memory.

The twelve black Mercedes that greeted us at the Hong Kong airport brought us safely to the family estate. During the next two days, large deliveries of cash followed, as our local leaders came in and discussed all the intelligence gathered on the competing Chinese families, with the aim of discovering who we thought was behind my assassination attempt. One family's members had made some claims to some people, taking credit for the attack, so we targeted their operations.

We recruited several dozen new mercenaries to carry out two simultaneous attacks. The family we targeted had a large chemical plant in Shenzhen, just across from the Hong Kong border. They also had a warehouse on the Hong Kong side of the border. First, we would attack the warehouse and set fire to it, drawing their attention as a diversion. Then we would launch a full-scale assault on the chemical plant, which we'd planned in great detail. All this preliminary work took place at a vacant warehouse on the outskirts of Hong Kong. No one was allowed to leave, and no cell phones or other communication devices were allowed. We didn't want any information leaking out about the attack. Then, once it was planned, the team was deployed for the attack that night. Meanwhile, security at all our Hong Kong and China facilities was quadrupled.

Father and I were escorted back to the family estate. We had a person stationed at a distance from each site who would send us live video. Once our teams arrived at their designated sites, the assault rifles and ammunition were handed out. Local delivery trucks were filled with the mercenaries, who quickly departed on their missions.

It was both surreal and exciting as we watched the live video coming in. The warehouse attack seemed to go fairly well. Once the flames became visible, Father celebrated and lit a Cuban cigar for each of us. The fire spread rapidly. Some of the chemicals must have been flammable because there were sounds of some small explosions, then the entire building went supernova. It was so hot, the firefighters couldn't get close to it. They just blocked off the surrounding area, trying to stop the fire from spreading to neighboring buildings.

Just then, the other, larger team assaulted the plant in China. That was a bloody battle, as this site was far better defended than the warehouse. For fifteen minutes, the fighting was intense as spurts of semiautomatic gunfire shot blasted through the video feed. After the gunshots quieted down, a couple of fires appeared on the video. Father and I celebrated again. This would be a major blow to that Chinese family that would last for many months, perhaps years. "An eye for an eye," Father said, as he proudly looked over at me.

"Well done, Father," I said. I had to admit he was right. The morale in our organization tripled afterward. Everyone felt that we were the top dog in the market. Father had a reputation, and now, so did I. There were now two White Tigers in Hong Kong.

Father was in a better mood the next day, so I told him, "I want to go and spend some time in LA. I need some time to process these important lessons."

He studied me for a moment, then said, "OK. This is probably a good time. The other families will take some time to lick their wounds and debate whether it's worth it to mess with us again. Either that, or it's going to escalate into World War Three right away. If that happens, I'll be here to handle it and you can come back."

I kept my mind focused on the events of the last few weeks to hide my excitement about seeing Jessica again. I hoped everything was OK. I wondered if she was still waiting for me and all my weirdness.

CHAPTER 7

I flew out of Hong Kong right away. The flight to LA seemed like an eternity. Once we landed, I went straight to where Jessica was working the last time I'd talked to her. The evening crowd was dying down when I walked in. She was taking an order, and then gave another table their check. She was preoccupied and didn't see me as I walked up behind her. When she finished with them, she turned around, gasped in surprise and dropped her notepad, then she squeaked loudly as we lunged into a tight bear hug. Tears streamed down our faces. The feeling of our connection, after having been apart for so long, was overwhelming. "I thought I'd lost you," she said.

"Never," I replied. Then I realized that she nearly did lose me.

She asked her manager and another server if they could take over for her, and we headed straight home. One of my two security guards was driving and the other was in the front passenger seat. I wanted to rip Jessica's clothes off right there, but we had to wait. Part of me was surprised she had waited for me – and yet, other than the longing, it seemed as though we had never been apart. We simply belonged with one another. "Do we need to stop for anything?" I asked her.

"Oh no. I want to be home with you NOW," she admitted with a smile and a wet kiss. I had always admired and loved how open and straightforward she was.

"Any chance you can speed us up?" I asked the driver with a smile.

"Yes, sir!" he said with a cheerful smile, instantly punching the accelerator to the floor. We were home in record time, and the guards let us in the front door. Holding her hand, I led her straight to the bedroom. We made love all night long, then watched the sun rise. It was a glorious morning with yellow, purple and pink clouds floating across the sky. I wished I could have frozen us in that moment so we could've stayed there forever.

I had a guard pick up a nice breakfast for us and we had breakfast in bed. We devoured it – and then each other – one more time. We lay there with me on my back and Jessica snuggled up against my right side for a long time. Then she said, "We need to talk," with some seriousness. I rolled onto my side, so that we were both lying there on our sides, looking into each other's eyes.

"OK," I said. "Let's talk. What's on your mind?" I asked.

"You know I love you. It's just… I can't do this anymore," she said.

"What do you mean?" I asked, shocked and surprised.

"You going away for ten months, without a word, without my knowing where you are, what you're doing, even if you're OK," she said. "I care for you so much. I worry about you. I can't stop thinking about you, so it makes me not want to think about you. I finally almost got to where I wasn't thinking about you as much, and then you showed up again."

"I feel the same way about you," I said softly. "It kills me to be cut off from you."

"When is this going to end?" she asked.

I had often asked myself the exact same question. "I don't know," I said.

"You have to confront him," she said.

"About us, you mean?" I asked.

"Yeeeesss," she said slowly, like it was obvious.

"I understand," I admitted. "Actually, it is so much more than just you and me. You would not believe what I went through this time. It was… horrible. People died. Lots of them." My eyes looked downward as a few of the moments flashed across my mind.

"Oh my God!" she said with surprise. I exhaled a big breath and rolled onto my back. "I'm sorry," she said softly. Then she snuggled up to me and kissed my cheek.

"It's so much different over there than here," I explained. "That's why Father has always spent more time over there, and I was safer here. It has been outright war in Hong Kong with some of the Chinese families. They even nearly killed me once." The surreal scenes played in my memory like a crazy action scene from a movie. My heart raced as I recalled all the sounds and feelings as I relived it briefly. "I don't want to go back," I confessed.

"Geez, how could you want to go back?" she asked empathetically. Her hand gently caressed my abdomen and chest as I lay there pondering our options.

"If I decided to run away, would you go with me?" I asked.

"You know I would," she said without hesitation. "We would be together all the time," she added.

"So much to think about," I said softly. I turned to her again and said, "I love you. You are my everything. There is nothing I would not do for you." I kissed her and caressed her cheek as her hand went from my chest to my stomach, then below. Soon we were making love again. God, she was so incredible. Our love was so incredible.

Later, the debate on what to do raged on in my mind. If I told Father about her, he would certainly be very unhappy. He would try to break us apart, without a doubt. Even if he somehow allowed us to stay together, I'd be stuck in the family business and all its ugliness. Worse, Jessica would be stuck in that life also. I thought of how sorry I felt for Mother. Then I thought of her advice that I shouldn't force things. Was confronting Father forcing things? Was running away forcing things? Damn it all.

A short two weeks of heaven passed when Father called me. "I need you back in Hong Kong ASAP," he said. "The plane will be there for you in the morning. Plan on seven AM." Then "Click."

Without thinking, I immediately called him back. My heart was racing. "Yes?" he asked.

"There's something I need to tell you," I said plainly.

"Really?" he said with some intrigue.

"I am in love, Father," I confessed.

"Must have been a hell of a two weeks!" he exclaimed.

"No," I admitted slowly. "It's been years now, actually."

"Really?" he said entirely differently this time, with disappointment and a touch of anger.

"Yes, Father," I replied. I paused for a deep breath before my full confession. "She is my soulmate. I want to marry her."

I had to put the phone at arm's length to save my eardrum from exploding due to the violent barrage of insults Father screamed into the phone. It sounded like he was literally frothing at the mouth like a rabid bloodhound. He said I had to end it immediately. He said he would cut me off from everything, and all I heard was "blah, blah, blah, blah, blah." I just didn't give a damn. The man had no idea of what love for another person was like. His heart was as cold as all of his stone hallways.

I waited for the barrage to stop, which took a few minutes. "She could travel with me to Hong Kong, India, wherever I'm needed," I said.

"You can have all the women you want everywhere you go," he said.

"I know, Father," I replied. "She's the only one I want anywhere."

"You will come to your senses," he said firmly. "Remember the lesson of your sixteenth birthday. I am cutting you off immediately." Then "Click!"

I tried calling back. He wouldn't answer. "Fine," I said out loud. "That went well," I joked to myself which garnered a little laughter and relief. Jessica came over after work and spent the night with me.

"I'm so proud of you," she said.

"I've really just been putting it off all this time," I admitted. "It certainly didn't make it any easier."

At exactly eight AM the next morning, the power went off at the house. I reached for my cell phone and it had no service. "Here we go," I said to Jessica, who was getting ready for work.

Luckily, I still had the prepaid cash cell phone I used for only Jessica. I pulled up my bank accounts. I no longer had access. Same with my credit cards. I felt the stress building on my chest like a great boulder.

"It's going to be OK," she said. "We don't need money to be happy, remember?" she reminded me.

"Thank you," I said kindly. "I know that's true. It's just going to be an interesting transition. Maybe this is the worst that will happen, and we'll actually be free," I said optimistically.

"Oh my God!" she said with a smile as she hugged and kissed me. "That would be so wonderful!" Then she said, "Hey baby, why don't you come on over to my place?" and gave me a sexy wink. I laughed at that idea. She was funny, and sexy. Remember the cash I began saving every week in college? I had continued that, so we did have a little nest egg, too.

I drove her to work with a security guard in the back. After I got back to the house, I let both the guards know that Father had cut me off. "I appreciate how you guys have protected Jessica and me all this time," I told them. "If I ever need you guys again, you will be the first ones I call." Of course they were disappointed to be losing the best gig they had ever had. All the time I was in Hong Kong and India, they were making big bucks just to guard an empty house. They understood, and said that they really appreciated me, too.

"You're by far the best boss we've ever had," said one of them, and the other agreed. "We'll come back to work for you in a second." I thanked them and they left. There I was in that moment, alone in my house on top of the hill. But for the first time in my life, I felt totally free. It was amazing. I thought of spending all my days with Jessica, and that warmth filled me up. I went inside and packed my things, and grabbed my two backpacks full of cash, excited for my new life. By the time I got out front to leave, someone had taken my BMW.

"Damn you, Father," I said exasperated. "You are thorough." I pulled out my cell phone and for the first time since college, I ordered an Uber ride, to Jessica's apartment. When I got there, she was at work. I took out my laptop and began working on my resume. I figured it would be easy to get a legal job, since so many firms had wanted me when I graduated Harvard. I contacted each of those firms and sent them my resume. Several weeks passed. I did not get a single call back. I applied for openings I found online with all the local firms. No calls back. Father was indeed thorough.

Jessica had never accepted any money from me. Her modest income was enough to pay for the apartment and food. We really had everything we needed. It was a very simple life. Our time together was amazing, and we got time together every single day. I was still adjusting, but we were happy. One beautiful summer Sunday, she had the day off so we went to the beach. I hadn't played in the water since college, so it was just what I needed. I reflected back on the helicopter ride with Father again, how no one was playing on the beach that beautiful sunny morning. I remembered my innocence, and how it didn't make any sense to me then. Then I remembered how I looked upon the common man as a slave. Over the past few years, I had realized that I, too, was a slave.

Playing with Jessica on the beach that day, and lying next to her underneath our little umbrella, I realized that she was the only person I had ever known who was truly free. If she was a slave to anything, it was to love, and I didn't think that love would have any slaves. She truly was my everything. I was the wealthiest man in the world. I truly was a king. As we watched the sun slowly sink into the ocean, I was sitting on my beach towel with her siting between my legs, leaning back against my chest. My arms were wrapped around her while I whispered sweet things in her ear. The sky turned yellow, then orange, then some purple and pink clouds lit up the sky as the sun disappeared inch by inch. It was perfect. I whispered into her sweet little ear, "You know I want to be with you forever."

"Yes!" she exclaimed, as tears poured out of her eyes. She flipped around and said, "You know I want to be with you forever too, Nigel" – then she pushed me onto my back and smothered me with hugs, kisses and loving tears. We laughed out of pure, exuberant joy. Everything was so amazing, so perfect. I had never been so happy. I could not imagine ever being happier.

We stopped by a small local grocery store on the way home and picked up a few things for dinner, plus some chocolate-covered strawberries and vanilla ice cream to celebrate. We playfully prepped dinner and as soon as we put it on the stove, we couldn't wait any longer. We stripped each other down. Then I lifted her up onto the kitchen countertop and things really got cooking, hotter than the pasta primavera steaming on the stove.

The pasta primavera and side salad were delicious, but both of us were looking forward to dessert. Soon, we took turns feeding each other bites of the chocolate-covered strawberries, which were pure heaven. Then we topped everything off with the ice cream before heading upstairs to the bedroom. The energy between us was always incredible. We had no problems staying up all night if we wanted to. We were lying there, snuggled up together, just kissing, talking and enjoying each other's company at two AM, when the Himalayan salt lamp on the nightstand suddenly shut off. Her phone was next to it charging, and the phone lit up.

"I think the power just shut off," I said softly. I got up and peeked out the window to see if the whole apartment complex and neighborhood had lost power. The lights were on in the parking lot, and I could see lights on around the apartment complex and in the neighborhood. "That's weird," I said. Then suddenly, glass from the window shattered as something whizzed by me and hit the wall behind me. I instantly dropped to the floor as the adrenaline exploded through my heart.

"Shit!" I yelled.

"What happened?" asked Jessica, not comprehending how the window had broken.

"Someone just shot at me!" I whispered loudly. "Get down and put your clothes on."

"Oh my God!" she whispered in shock. Finding our clothes was easy. Scrambling to put them on in the pitch-black dark was a challenge. I shimmied into my pants while lying on the floor, then we heard loud crashes on the apartment's front door downstairs. They were kicking in the door. I found my backpack and grabbed my pistol. I realized how stupid I was to not have any spare clips of ammo as I quickly slid the safety off and scooted toward the bedroom doorway. From there I could barely see through the dark apartment. Fortunately, a faint light was coming through the downstairs windows.

The front door vibrated with each booming impact. The door was about to give way as I crouched and aimed chest-level into the doorway. I could feel my heart beating, but it was as though I was watching a silent movie. I sensed everything around me. My focus in that moment was intense as Jessica squeezed up behind me along the wall. One more "boom" on the front door and it nearly gave, as the doorframe's wood splintered around the locks.

The next kick easily flung the front door wide open as two men dressed all in black came through. "Bang! Bang!" my gun blasted out as the two bodies slumped to the ground in the doorway. Then a gun and a black-sleeved arm appeared from the side of the doorway and unloaded its clip in random directions. I waited patiently. As he reloaded, another gun appeared and unloaded its clip, so I knew there were at least two of them.

There was a momentary pause, then a head bobbed quickly in and out, trying to identify my location without success. Then one gun appeared again, firing in all directions as another man came flying over the two bodies lying in the doorway. His abdomen caught my next bullet and he crashed to the ground, grabbing his stomach with both hands, as the next man in black came flying in. "Bang!" went my gun. "Shit! I missed him," I thought. He rolled into the kitchen behind the cabinets. I panned over to catch him as he popped up, when suddenly another man flew through the front doorway.

"Bang!" went my gun again toward the front door. I hit him in the thigh, which I knew wasn't good enough. In the corner of my eye I saw the man in black pop up in the kitchen and I knew it was time to hit the floor. "Down!" I yelled to Jessica as the gunshots blasted outward from downstairs, easily splintering the doorjamb and piercing the drywall above us as easily as tissue paper. I thought, "One, two, three, four, yeah four," as I counted the number of shots I had fired. I knew that I had just nine bullets. "Idiot!" I chided myself for my naivety. I bobbed my head up quickly, then squirmed forward to check on the status of the men downstairs.

I couldn't see the man I hit in the leg, so he had moved in closer. It felt like the other man was still in the kitchen as I sat there in the silence. The sound of sirens appeared in the far-off distance. I realized this only put pressure on them to hurry up, so I set my aim on the kitchen and waited. I had guessed wrong, as a man jumped out at the bottom of the stairs and opened fire. Again I went down to the floor. "Bang! Bang! Bang! Bang!" rang the gunshots.

I quickly popped my head up and down as the man in the kitchen fired three more shots that zinged just above my head. I hurled myself into a sideways roll. "Damn! That was close," I thought. "Go peek out the window," I whispered to Jessica as I pointed my gun backward. Then I fixed my aim toward the stairs. "Don't leave your head in plain sight." To my surprise, just then several gunshots went off directly below me, as bullets shot upward through the floor around me. I burst into another roll toward the bed and crashed into the footboard, then refocused my aim on the stairs. The sounds of sirens were a little closer.

"I don't see anything," whispered Jessica, looking at me while crouched down below the corner of the window.

"OK," I whispered backwards without looking, focused on the stairway. Then I thought arrogantly as I waited for them, "If you want the White Tiger, come and get me." It was eerily silent in the apartment at that moment. Dogs were barking in the adjacent neighborhood as the sirens approached. I heard the familiar wood creak at the bottom of the stairs, and I knew they were coming. A long ten or fifteen seconds slowly ticked by, when a gun popped up from below the floor's level on the stairs and began firing. "Bang!" went my gun, and the gun and hand went flying backward as the man screamed in pain, followed by what sounded like him tumbling down the stairs.

Another really long pause in the silence followed. Another gun popped up and quickly fired three shots, then his head popped up. "Bang!" went my gun. Instant lobotomy. The sirens were nearer now, as I lay there waiting, ever focused on the stairway. Time crawled by in the stillness.

"The police are here!" Jessica whispered with relief.

"Stay down!" I said. "Wait for them to come to us." The bodies and blood in the broken doorway formed an easy road sign for the policemen as the parking lot filled up with red and blue flashing lights. One after another, I heard each car's siren turn off as its engine revved into the parking lot, tires screeching to a stop. All the red and blue lights flashed across our once-dark bedroom walls. Then I heard sounds of their car doors opening and quickly slamming shut as all the policemen got out of their cars and crouched behind the engine blocks with their guns pointed over the hood. The parking lot was loaded with erect testosterone, eager to unload. I could feel the tenseness in the air.

"Bang!" a gunshot went off from downstairs. "Oh my God," was all I could think as all the policemen immediately opened fire. Jessica dove down toward me on the floor. We clung with our lives to the bedroom floor as a couple dozen cops emptied a couple clips into the apartment. Chips of drywall and paint rained down on us. Glass from the windows sprayed over us as the bullets shattered lights, blasted pictures off the walls and burst pipes. The gunfire lasted for what seemed like forever, but it was probably only a minute or so. A deafening silence followed. Jessica and I were shaking and frozen. I don't even remember breathing that entire time. "Great. Now we have a parking lot full of trigger-happy cops," I thought.

"Come out with your hands up!" boomed the command from the megaphone outside. I still wasn't sure if all the men in black were dead downstairs. After all, a gunshot had just been fired from down there.

"What should we do?" whispered Jessica in a panic.

"I'm thinking," I whispered back. In my mind I asked, "How do we get out of this without getting killed?" I pondered it for a while. "I have to keep my eyes on the stairs still," I whispered. "Go to the window. Don't show yourself. Yell "Don't shoot!"

She looked at me like I was insane. "Trust me," I said. She gave me a look, then slowly crawled over to below the bedroom window overlooking the parking lot.

"Don't shoot!" her nervous voice rang out through the silence. Immediately, thick beams of bright white light shot through the window. "Now what do I do?" she asked in a panic.

I answered quickly, "Say, 'Don't shoot!' again. Ever so slowly, lift your palms up into the light of the window."

"Don't shoot!" she yelled, even more nervously than the first time. "Please!" she pleaded. "Don't shoot!" her shaking palms slowly appeared in the illuminated window.

"Come out so we can see you," commanded the strong, masculine voice from the parking lot as all of their guns focused on the window.

I felt Jessica look back at me, so I glanced back at her, nodded and said, "Very slowly. It'll be OK." I quickly turned back toward the stairs and prayed with everything I had that it actually would be OK. She slowly continued raising her hands and arms, and then her messy, gorgeous brunette hair and fear-filled face slowly appeared in the window.

"Keep your hands up and don't move," commanded the voice. Jessica simply nodded that she understood.

"What happened?" asked the strong voice.

"We were attacked!" Jessica yelled.

"Come out with your hands up!" commanded the voice.

She shook her head "No." "We don't know if it's safe downstairs," she explained. This kicked off a great discussion in the parking lot, as Jessica sat there in the spotlight and I held my gun toward the stairs.

We waited for at least fifteen minutes, which seemed like eternity, before the voice responded again. "OK. Do not move or you will be shot. Do you understand?"

"Yes," Jessica yelled, adding a strong up-and-down nod.

Many more minutes crawled by as I sat there, one with the floor. Then finally, news came from Jessica, who turned her head very slowly toward me. She whispered, "The SWAT team is coming in."

"Now this is progress," I thought with some relief. "Finally." We waited patiently as the SWAT team moved in. I heard the bodies in the doorway being dragged outside. Then some quick movements of multiple men downstairs. "Freeze," many of them yelled at different points, seemingly as they approached the men in black. "This one's dead," I heard. Then, "This one's dead, too." I heard the sounds of all the doors, even the cabinets being opened and closed. "Kitchen is clear!" announced one of them in a strong voice. Then other voices yelled "Clear!" "Clear here!" "Clear!" "All clear downstairs."

The voice from the parking lot commanded "Come down with your hands up. It is all clear downstairs."

"OK!" Jessica backed up as she started bawling. She turned slowly toward me. I nodded, and released a huge exhale. I set my gun on the floor and got up as she slowly backed up from the window. We embraced in such a strong hug, squeezing each other like never before, thankful to be alive.

"Come down with your hands up!" commanded another masculine voice from downstairs.

"OK!" Jessica yelled.

"OK!" I yelled, too. I slowly approached the stairs with my arms stretched to the sky above me. Jessica followed a few feet behind me.

As I cautiously stepped through the doorway, several flashlights blinded my eyes from downstairs. I squinted, trying to see the steps below me. There were at least a dozen assault rifles focused on me. "Please, don't shoot," I said calmly. "Thank you." Tears started streaming down my face as I slowly took one step at a time.

"Please, don't shoot," said Jessica as she started down the stairs behind me.

When I reached the bloody bottom of the stairs, one of them said, "Put your hands behind your head," which I did. Then I was commanded to drop to my knees. I did so, then I was pushed to the floor and handcuffed. They did the same with Jessica. Looking around the flashing red and blue apartment, the policemen's flashlights and white lights beaming from the parking lot illuminated all the holes, bodies, blood, glass and debris littering the once-beautiful apartment. I saw that the last man in black had blown his brains out rather than being caught alive. Four of the five men looked Chinese, so I figured it was a visit from my Hong Kong friends. We were put in separate police cars and hauled downtown to the police station for our statements and questioning. Late that afternoon, they let us go.

Even if we had wanted to, we couldn't stay at the apartment. It was a major crime scene. All of the bullets were being logged as evidence. My gun was confiscated, and so were my two backpacks full of cash. We were able to grab some clothes, those that didn't have bullet holes, and pack a few things.

Jessica had a little money in her bank account and a couple of credit cards, so we checked in and paid cash for a cheap motel on the east side of town while we figured things out. That evening and night I spent comforting Jessica, who cried almost non-stop. Ironically, I was pretty much fine. I couldn't help but smirk at the insanity of it, but Father was right. Apparently, you do get used to nearly being killed.

CHAPTER 8

I wasn't sure what to do next. I pondered going to the family estate for help. I knew how that would go. I could call Jack or Elliot and see if they could help me with a job or a place to stay. Most of all, I was concerned for Jessica's safety. Me getting killed was one thing, but this time SHE nearly got killed. That part of it broke my heart. I asked myself, "How could we be together and be safe?" I had no idea how they had found me in the first place. The apartment was in Jessica's name, so now she would be a target, too. The more I thought about it, I really only had two options: wait to get my cash back, then run far away to an isolated place, or go back to Father and somehow get us both under his protection, which did not seem likely.

After we made love first thing in the morning, Jessica rubbed her hand on my chest and said, "Let's go play on the beach." At first I thought she was joking, and then I remembered her genius. Then she reminded me, "You know more than anyone else how this world works. You are my king. You will figure this out. The answer will come to you." I remembered my mother's advice to not force things.

I rolled over and pressed my body against hers. I looked her in the eyes and said, "You are so beautiful and so amazing, my love." I kissed her sweetly. "Yes, let's go play on the beach."

We surfed for two hours that morning, rising and falling with the cold waves in the warm sun, smiling, laughing and enjoying the moment. I remembered again how simple life was, and how little we needed to be happy. We brought our boards in and curled up on the warm sand to thaw out. Over the course of the day, a new option presented itself – one that Father would have been proud of. Snuggled up watching the sunset, I told Jessica, "I have an idea, finally."

"Do I want to know what it is?" she asked softly.

"No," I responded.

"I thought that's what you'd say," she said. "I trust you. I love you." That was the end of the discussion.

We spent three more days on the beach, living and loving life together, before I made the decision. I wanted to make sure my mind and heart were clear. It was obvious to me that this new option was what I would pursue. It was dangerous, but I was a desperate man in love. I had become the most dangerous creature in the world.

I knew a lot about the Chinese family that we had retaliated heavily against in Hong Kong. I had been intimately involved in all of the intelligence briefings. I knew I could get in touch with them. With the attack in Jessica's apartment, I knew I had their attention. I went online and researched their businesses and their boards of directors. I found the man I wanted. I handwrote my message to him in Mandarin. It simply said, "I have an offer I think you will find very attractive. I ask for one short phone call. Please email me with a phone number and time to call." I signed it as "The Young White Tiger," and left a brand-new email address that I had set up just for this. I mailed it from LA to his attention at his company's headquarters in Hong Kong. Then I waited.

Jessica and I decided to head south, just to distance ourselves from Los Angeles. I expected to be able to get my cash from the police within sixty days, so we just had to stretch what she had until then. Three weeks later, the answer to my email arrived. I was to call him the following Monday at ten AM Hong Kong time.

Monday arrived in a flash. I drove up to LA just to find a payphone to make the call. Without hesitation he asked, "What is your offer?"

"You know that my father has cast me out, yes?" I asked.

134

"Yes," he replied matter-of-factly.

"I know that you want the White Tiger out of Hong Kong, yes?" I asked.

"Yes," he answered.

"My proposal is to give us both what we want," I said, and then paused for effect. He waited silently. "I will give you my father. You will then buy my Hong Kong business from me for a reasonable price. It is the most profitable business in our portfolio. Then the White Tiger will be out of Hong Kong forever." I knew that compared to the high costs of waging war, this was an attractive proposal.

A long silence followed. My palms were sweating as my heart galloped. Finally, he said, "Let me consider this." Then "Click." He hung up the phone.

"That was kind of like talking to Father," I thought. It was nearly impossible to read him over the phone, but I felt it was an offer he would not refuse.

The next month passed by slowly. I began to wonder if my offer had been refused, when finally my phone pinged me that I had received an email. I opened it up to find another scheduled phone call, which was definitely progress.

"What are the specifics of your proposal?" he asked.

"I want two million cash up front and a guarantee of safety for me and my woman," I stated plainly.

"That is a lot of money," he replied.

"Not for you," I reminded him. "Think of it as a very small down payment on the business."

"What will you do for me?" he asked.

"I will re-join my father's organization. Then I will let you know a time and place where you can eliminate him," I explained.

"How do I know you just won't take over the business?" he asked.

"You don't," I answered, because it was true. "But I assure you, it is not my intention. I don't care much for Hong Kong. If you have other businesses elsewhere, this could be the start of a powerful partnership."

"I will consider it," he replied. Then, "Click!"

"Well, there it is," I thought. It would be a long wait until my phone notified me of a new email two weeks later.

I took a few deep breaths and long exhales before I opened the message. There was another phone call scheduled. This was it.

"I accept your offer," he said. "You have six months to deliver the goods, or I will have your head on a plate."

"I need twelve months," I responded. "I need time to regain Father's trust."

A torturously long silence followed, the he said, "Very well. Twelve months from today."

"Perfect," I agreed.

"Call this phone number to get your cash," he said, and then he gave me a local phone number.

"Got it," I said.

"A pleasure," he said.

"Thank you," I replied. And the call was over.

I called up my two former security guards and told each of them, "We're back in business!" The three of us met for my call to make the arrangements to get the two million dollars. The cash transfer was set up in a busy park on Saturday afternoon. One of my guards went in my place to grab the backpack full of cash in case it was a bomb or a setup. They met in the dark shade of a tall tree. After he verified it was the cash, he transferred it to his own backpack in case there was a tracking device on the original backpack, which he stuffed into a garbage can. Making sure he wasn't followed in and out of a few different busy places, he made his way back to us. It was a success. We were indeed back in business.

To keep Jessica safe, I paid cash under a fictitious identity for a small cabin up the coast in Oregon so that she would still have access to the ocean. Both security guards had no issues keeping an eye on her up there. I told them I had a year to deliver my promise for the two million, so that it would not be forever.

Then it was time for the next part of the plan, one that I found much more challenging. I had to call Father and apologize, and ask him to take me back. This meant telling him I had broken it off with Jessica. I realized it was far easier for me to be an honest villain than a liar.

I picked up a new prepaid cash cell phone in LA. I input Father's number and texted him, "It's me, Father. You win. Please accept me back. Call me." A week went by with no answer. Then two weeks, three, four, then eight. I was getting nervous about the whole head-on-a-plate thing, although they had been trying to kill me any way so what was I really risking. Finally, Father called me back.

"Why should I take you back?" he asked coldly.

"I'm your son, Father. You have invested much in me to continue your kingdom," I answered.

"And the woman?" he asked.

"I had no choice," I said. "I had to let her go. I nearly got her killed in her LA apartment a while back. I couldn't afford to protect her, and she couldn't take the stress."

"Yes. I heard about that," he said rather unhappily. "You have no idea how much it takes to suppress a story of a billionaire's son involved in an LA shootout that left five dead. Our pictures would have been in newspapers everywhere."

"Ohhhh," I uttered, realizing what he was saying.

"All your life, I've tried to get you to realize WHO you are," he added. "If a king walks among the common people, there will always be someone who wants to kill him."

I looked down at the floor as I heard him say those words. I didn't want it to be true, but its truth was now obvious. "I think I understand that, finally," I admitted.

"Good," he said simply. "I'll be at the LA estate on Saturday. Be there at eight AM."

"Yes, Father," I said. He hung up before I could say, "Thank you."

"That went well," I thought. "Everything is going according to plan, assuming he indeed takes me back in.

Saturday will be interesting." It was time to let Jessica know that I'd be going away for a while. This time, we made plans to keep in touch online. She set up a couple of fake social media accounts. I also memorized the cabin's address so that I could drop something in the mail if I got a chance.

I spent as much time as possible with Jessica the rest of the week. Thursday night, I was lying in bed, pressed up against her in our usual position. I ran my fingers through her long, soft, dark hair and kissed her. "This is the last time we will be apart," I told her softly. Then I said, "It's going to be dangerous. If a few months go by and you haven't heard from me, I want you to take the money and move on. If I'm dead, there won't be any reason for anyone to come after you." She didn't like that. She rolled away from me and her body began convulsing as she cried heavily. I snuggled up behind her, trying to comfort her.

"I never could have imagined all of this," she said in between hard cries. "Almost every night, I have nightmares about that night in the apartment. The gunshots. The breaking glass. The bullets whizzing by me and destroying everything. The blood. The bodies. The glass and debris falling on me. The fear of dying. And worst of all, the fear of losing you." She cried heavily again, then she added. "I worry about you all the time. ALL the time! EVERY time you leave,

I wonder if I'm ever going to see you again. It's so terrible." She broke down crying. For the first time, I felt her suffering as a river flooded down my face. I could see that I had become so desensitized. A dark and heavy guilt crept into my heart. I realized that I had been totally absent for her in this way. Feeling her pain in that moment crushed my soul.

"I am SO sorry," was all I could say, then I held her as we cried together for the longest time. Eventually, the tears subsided, and I pulled her top shoulder back, asking her to roll over and face me.

"I love you so much," I said softly as I gently held her cheek. "You've already saved me. You saved me from a life of not living, from a life of becoming my father. Nothing can break a love such as ours. Remember, love conquers all."

"I love you, too," she said as she pulled me tight. "I've never seen you cry," she added. "You have no idea how much it means to me, to see that you care so much for me. You're such a beautiful man." Then she started caressing my chest with her hand as she looked deep into my eyes. The connection between us was incredible. I was so open for her in that moment. I had never been so turned on in my life. In seconds, we were making sweet love like never before.

When I woke that morning, my arms were still wrapped around her from behind. I never wanted to move again, feeling her warmth, inhaling and exhaling softly with her. Right there, I had all that I could have possibly wanted in life. I lay there for an hour, just taking her in. Then it was time to get up and get ready to catch my flight. I had made a deal with the devil. There was no turning back.

As I slowly disentangled my arms from Jessica, she woke up. As I started to get out of bed, she pulled me back in. "I don't want you to go," she said softly.

"I know," I replied. I turned and looked into her beautiful brown eyes and said, "Trust me, I don't want to go either." I caressed her cheek and kissed her softly. "This will be the last time we're apart." We just stared into each other's eyes for a few moments, silently conveying all that could have possibly been said, then I rolled over and out of bed. A quick shave and shower, then I threw the last few things in my suitcase and we said our goodbyes. I watched her watch me drive away.

CHAPTER 9

The cabin was in a remote location, so it took nearly three hours to get to the airport. My flight was on time and everything was going smoothly. My thoughts were consumed by the task ahead of me. Father was truly a master at many things, and he was ruthless. I would have to be incredibly patient and play my plan of betrayal to absolute perfection. I decided I would clear my mind of any thoughts of betrayal for quite some time. I would simply focus on being his loyal and abiding son, waiting for the opportunity to present itself.

In Los Angeles, Father's driver was waiting for me at the baggage claim. "It's good to see you, young master," he said warmly.

"It's very good to see you, too," I said with a warm smile. He always had maintained a pleasant attitude, which for many was difficult around Father. Sitting in the back of the black Mercedes, I noticed my palms were sweating. "Breathe, damnit," I commanded myself. "Everything's going to be fine." Then I thought of Jessica and replayed our incredible connection and lovemaking from the night before. "My God, what a woman," I thought, and her warmth filled me to the brim. Right then I realized I had found my power, my inspiration. Jessica's love would power me through the darkest depths of hell and back again. She was the light that would guide me home. I would not fail her.

As the car rolled up to the estate, the large wrought-iron gate parted in the middle and swung open. A guard eyed us as we glided by, and I quietly let out a big exhale as the main house came into view. Two security guards greeted us at the front door, which was unusual. One of them took my bags toward my room. I said goodbye to the driver; then I was informed that Father was waiting for me in his study. The second security guard escorted me down the familiar large stone-floored hallways to the study. He opened the door and held it open for me to enter.

As I came through the doorway, I saw Father sitting behind his large, dark mahogany desk. "Hello, Father," I said, as warmly as I possibly could. He just stared coldly at me as I walked to the front of the desk and sat down in the dark leather chair. I met his gaze and stared blankly at him, waiting for what would happen next. He said nothing as his eyes searched the depths of my soul. "I'm sorry, Father," I confessed. "You warned me about the dangers of a woman, and I let a woman come between us. I am sorry."

"All this, for a woman!" Father yelled, as he angrily smashed his fist onto his desk. "Do you see how just one woman can destroy you? Destroy your family? Your kingdom?" He paused his rage to make sure I acknowledged him. "So many women are simply waiting at your fingertips, yet you attached to one. Do you see how stupid this was?" I nodded. "You nearly got yourself killed! And that cost me a small fortune, covering up a story of a billionaire's son involved in a shootout with the LA police. They fired nearly four hundred rounds!" He chuckled amidst his anger as he imagined the scene and repeated, "Four hundred fucking rounds!" Then he added, a little more softly, "Unbelievable!"

My eyes looked downward as I recalled that night in the apartment. The bangs on the door, the men breaking in, the gunfight, the gun-holding hand flying off, the man's head splattering like a melon, and then all the gunshots and bullets whizzing past from the parking lot. Then I remembered Jessica, her nightmares and fears and how hard she cried on our last night together. It was all so terrible. "It was terrible," I muttered aloud.

I looked up at Father with what I imagined to be huge, sad puppy eyes, hoping for an ounce of compassion. "You look pathetic!" he yelled, angrily pounding his fist again onto the desk. "You are a king!" He paused for emphasis, then repeated, "A king!" His chest heaved from the rage and heavy breathing as the adrenaline pumped through his veins, one of which was now bulging on the left side of his forehead. I had never seen him so angry.

"I'm sorry, Father," I said much more firmly than the first time. He sat there and studied me for a while.

"The woman made you soft, do you see?" he asked. I nodded. This was a definite truth. "Remember Hong Kong," he said. "The White Tigers are not soft. We can never be seen as soft! Do you understand?"

"Yes. I understand," I answered quickly. He was definitely right from a business point of view. There was no questioning Father's effectiveness in Hong Kong, or anywhere else.

"Your whole life, have you ever seen me as soft?" he asked pointedly.

"Absolutely not, Father," I quickly replied. He paused and studied me again as his breathing slowed a bit.

"We must eradicate this softness from you," he said. "Or it will destroy you. Only the strong survive. The weak are devoured by the strong. There is no mercy in the business of conquerors. Do you understand?"

"I understand, Father," I replied firmly while nodding my head. He stared and studied me for a minute.

"What is the most dangerous creature in the world?" Father asked.

"It is definitely a woman," I responded.

"Do not forget it again," he said quickly and coldly. "For the next few weeks, my business advisors will bring you up to speed on what has happened in each business around the world since you've been gone, including what the situation was and how I handled it. Keep your evenings free." Then he gestured toward the door, indicating it was time for me to leave.

"Got it," I said. Then I got up and walked out, closing the door behind me. I released a big exhale as I walked down the hallway. At first, I wondered if I could really do this. But I quickly remembered Jessica, and my resolve hardened like granite. The head butler intercepted me on my way back to my room and informed me that my first meeting was in thirty minutes. He asked me if I wanted anything and I responded that I was fine.

The first business advisor brought a stack of papers with him. He had printed emails and other business documents to recreate each situation that had arisen. My homework was to study each situation and propose our action or decision, then I would be informed of what Father had done and we would compare and analyze the two. Father had several business advisors, so this process was going to take weeks.

Meanwhile, dinner each evening was from six to seven PM. At seven o'clock sharp every night, a different flavor of beautiful woman arrived to entertain me. Father was intent at proving his point that women were a dime a dozen, but I felt sorry for him that he had never experienced a love like Jessica and I had. It was such a twisted feeling to have to make love to other women on my journey toward the one woman my soul longed for. I had to wall off my feelings for Jessica just to keep myself together. I could not be seen as soft. Two months swiftly passed until Father sent me to Hong Kong.

In Hong Kong, the seven PM routine continued. I grabbed the reins of the business while Father traveled the globe greasing wheels, pulling puppet strings and taking care of other business. The chemical business flowing from China through Hong Kong was stronger than ever, but we had started to experience some losses again. One truck two weeks ago did not make it to the warehouse and then this week, two trucks disappeared after leaving the warehouse. The drivers also disappeared, so we assumed they were dead or had defected to the Chinese.

After multiple briefings, we defined standard delivery routes. We placed a small army along the delivery routes in cars and small cargo trucks. Each vehicle had a person designated to communicate any action via cell phone. Then we placed GPS trackers on each delivery truck and we gave them an emergency button to hit at the first sign of trouble. One person always monitored the trucks' GPS to identify unexpected stoppages and route changes. I didn't want to randomly target the other families and rekindle war unnecessarily. I wanted to catch the culprits red-handed and then deal with them. "Just bring in one or two alive," was all that I asked.

The plan went live on a Tuesday, and on Friday we got our first emergency button notification. The armed guards immediately sped toward the truck, which thirty seconds later moved off the delivery route. Back at the estate, we had a war room set up with a full wall of monitors. I watched the GPS blip turn off the delivery route, and I could see our five cars full of armed guards converging on the truck. Turn by turn, we talked to the armed guards live via cell phone on a conference call.

Two minutes later, two of our cars were just a few cars back at a light that had just turned red, ready to converge. "Wait!" I ordered. "Stay back. Let's see where the truck is going." One of my men in the control room had been a taxi driver in Hong Kong for twenty years. He knew the city like the back of his hand. We also knew some of our competitors' locations.

Traffic was heavy, so it would have been nearly impossible for the truck driver to pick up that he was being followed. There were cars everywhere stuck in the same traffic. I ordered our other cars to take parallel routes, in case the truck turned and our cars behind him got stuck behind a red light. Ten minutes later, the truck made a turn, and then turned into a multiple-floor warehouse. The warehouse had a large, spiraling cement ramp for trucks to drive up, until they reached the correct floor for that company's warehouse. One guard told me the warehouse looked about twenty floors high.

"Go in after him," I ordered. Two of our cars drove onto the ramp about thirty seconds behind the truck, which was already out of sight up and around the bend. A minute later, two other cars made it to the ramp with the fifth car speeding toward them.

The communicator in the first car announced each floor as they went higher and looked for our missing truck. "Not on two. Not on three. Not on four. Not on five. Not on six. Not on seven. Not on eight. It's on nine! The truck got off on nine!" The car stayed back as the driver peeked up and around at our truck as it went further into the warehouse on that floor. "What do you want us to do, Boss?" they asked.

"We have your two cars, plus two cars coming up the ramp maybe a minute behind you, and then another car," I advised them. "Wait for the next two cars to arrive behind you. Then I want all of you to speed in there, surprise them, and kill them all. Bring our truck back, and don't leave any of our people or bodies behind. Understand?"

"Yes, Boss," was the short reply.

"Find out who they are. Take pictures of them. If there's any paperwork in there showing the name of the company, take a picture or bring me the paper," I added.

"OK, Boss. Got it," he responded quickly. Thirty seconds ticked by slowly, then he said, "We're going in now." He put the phone on speaker as he grabbed his gun. I heard the engine shift into drive as the car crept up to the warehouse floor, then I heard all the windows roll down. Suddenly the engine roared as tires screeched, echoing off the warehouse walls, and I heard the other cars behind them follow suit. A dozen gunshots blasted through the cell phones with incredible echoes bouncing back and forth amid sounds of men yelling. Then there was another handful of gunshots, a delay, and then one final "Bang!" echoed through the warehouse.

"It's over, Boss. They were definitely not expecting us. Just six or seven warehouse workers. A huge success," he said.

"Yes!" I yelled voraciously and thrust a fist into the air. "That'll teach those bastards! Find me some papers," I ordered. "What's in the warehouse?" I asked.

"There's a large tanker truck here, and a couple of smaller tanks," he said. "They must have been draining our trucks into the big one."

"Hurry and take pictures and grab documents. Then torch it and get the team out," I ordered.

"Yes, Boss," he replied quickly. Two and a half minutes later, our cars and truck were rolling out and down the ramp as the big truck was engulfed in flames, setting off the fire alarm and sprinklers throughout the warehouse. Later, I was informed that our truck driver's bloody body was on the truck's passenger-side floor, with a bullet hole in his chest and out his back.

I was invigorated by the successful operation. The young White Tiger had taken an eye for an eye. Two weeks later, no more trucks had disappeared. We left the GPS trackers on our delivery trucks and kept monitoring them, but I called the armed-guard patrols off. Afterward, when Father had found out about everything, he called me. I answered, saying, "Hello, Father."

"Now, THAT'S my son," was all that he said before hanging up. I felt good. I felt so powerful, like a king. I looked forward to my seven PM appointment that night and thought, "Whoever my personal shopper is, they're doing one hell of a job." I did have a special thing for Asian women. They seemed so elegant with their perfect skin; long, shiny black hair and those amazing dark and narrow eyes. It was a total turn-on.

As I walked down a long hallway, I caught a glimpse of myself in a mirror. Suddenly, I stopped in my tracks as my conscience and reality slapped me in the face. I realized I was already five months into my deal with the devil and my thoughts turned to Jessica. "I'm turning into my father again," I admitted. I could feel the money, power and sex consuming me. I rubbed both palms of my hands up and down my face. I pondered for the millionth time why a child always wanted to please a parent that he hated. Damn it all.

CHAPTER 10

The next month flew by, as nothing bad happened in Hong Kong. Then Father had me fly to the UK to take care of some business there for a couple weeks. Then I went to LA to take care of some things for a week. Jessica seemed like a distant memory. I thought about trying to sneak up to Oregon and see her, but it just wasn't worth the risk. If I got caught, all would be lost. Father had my schedule filled anyway. All I managed was a quick letter in the mail telling her everything was OK, that I missed her and would be with her soon.

Soon it was time for the young White Tiger to return to Hong Kong. Due to the always-possible turmoil, we had to maintain a strong presence there to keep up the morale and loyalty of the men. I had not seen Father since my initial return in LA. He liked the idea of the two of us always being in different places so that we could each run the business in that location. Soon I was eight months into my deal, then nine months. I had barely checked in with Jessica. I somersaulted deeper into the abyss of sex, power and money as I pondered embezzling two million dollars to pay it back and cancel the deal, if that was even possible. I was sure I could pull it off without Father missing the money.

After being in Hong Kong for two weeks, my cell phone rang. It was my man in charge of Hong Kong. His Chinese name, which started with X, was a difficult one to say in English, so we just called him X or X-man. "I have some bad news," he said. "The warehouse near the port was just hit. It's on fire. I'm assuming none of our men got out. The fire department has just arrived and is trying to stop the fire from spreading."

"Damn it!" I yelled as I punched the wall next to where I was standing. My left hand held the cell phone while my stinging right hand massaged my forehead as I searched my thoughts for what to do next. I knew that we would have to hit them back even harder, and far worse, I had to call Father. I felt like throwing up as the waves of stress rocked my stomach. "Alert all the men," I instructed him. "Triple all security right now at every location. We have a lot of work to do." Then, "Click!" I hung up the phone.

This was a far more serious loss than anything I had experienced. I stared at my phone in my hand, debating whether to put off calling Father to give him the news. "Might as well get it over with," I admitted. "It's not like I'll be able to think about anything else." I found Father's number at the top of my favorites and tapped it. It seemed like it took forever to connect and hear the first ring.

"Yes?" Father answered, seeming annoyed.

"I have some news, Father," I said firmly. "The warehouse near the port was just hit and torched. Probably all the men are lost." I may have seemed calm on the outside, but inside everything was twisting into a tight ball, cringing for what would come next. It was silent for a few moments, but I could feel the steam rising within Father.

"Those mother fuckers have the balls to fuck with us again!" he yelled from a deep place through gritted teeth. "Unbelievable! They know this is going to result in all-out war." A long silence followed, then he continued. "This is your fault. They must perceive you as weak. They never would have fucked with me like this." I felt this like a punch in the gut, and all the air left me as I struggled to find my breath. Another silence followed as the chain reaction exploded through my body.

Father added, "I will be there in two days. Have the men gather the intelligence, and hire another hundred men. We're going to hit them hard, hit their families, and keep hitting them." Then "Click!" The call was over.

"That went well," I chided myself as all my energy drained out of me. The stress was overwhelming. I took a few minutes to gather enough strength to call X-man back.

"Yes, Boss?" he answered.

I replied coldly, "Father will be here in two days. Find out who did this, and recruit another hundred men." Then "Click!"

I replayed Father's words over and over in my mind, "This is your fault. They must perceive you as weak." Then I thought, "He's such an asshole." I sat down and slumped forward with both hands on my forehead. "He's always been an asshole." I pondered my dilemma, and then I remembered my deal. "On the positive side, this may be the opportunity I've been waiting for." Deep within, a spark of hope ignited a flame. I remembered my angel waiting to welcome me from this hell. "This is it," I told myself with a new-found resolve.

That night, I had a couple of security guards escort me off the estate so I could drop a couple of items in the mail. One was a letter to Jessica, telling her how much I loved and missed her, and that hope was still alive. The other letter simply said, "Be ready," and instructed him to text me from a number I could communicate with discreetly.

The next forty-eight hours were hectic, as backpacks of cash rolled out of the estate to buy information. We hired a hundred and thirty more men. Everything had to be in order before Father arrived. Two nights later, from the second-floor study's window, I watched Father and his security escort roll into the estate. I let out a long, deep breath, trying to blow out all my anxiety. Then I got up and headed down to greet Father.

I was almost to the front door as one of the men swung it open. Father burst through and simply ordered, "Come," as he stormed past me. He was on a mission. I followed closely behind him as our footsteps echoed through the great stone hallways, and then up the stairs through the long wooden hallway that was like an Oriental art gallery, until we reached the study. He sat at the front edge of his seat, clasped his hands together and asked me, "So, what do we know?"

"It looks like it was not the last family that hit us, but rather two other families: The Red Dragons and the Black Serpents," I informed him. "I don't know if they are colluding with the first family and simply taking turns, but we know that the men who torched the warehouse were working for these two families."

"Damn Chinese," he said angrily. "They are all in it together, whether formally or not. The last family probably did not want to incur any more losses until they've recovered from our last hit."

I said in a business-like tone, "X is prepared to give us a full debrief. We have refreshed the intelligence on where their business operations are and where some of the family members live. I have men assigned to watch movements of each person we've identified to look for vulnerabilities and learn more. We're set up in the library to use the big conference table to lay out all the information."

"What about our existing operations?" Father asked.

"We have tripled the security everywhere," I replied. "Security is on constant full alert. I have an armed guard riding with every delivery truck."

"I want to review how many guards we have at each location and where they are stationed," he said. "Particularly at our largest remaining facilities. I don't want to lose another big facility."

"Yes, Father," I replied. "I will get that for you right away." I texted X to get that information.

"Good," he said. "As soon as I have that, I want to tour each facility tomorrow."

"Yes, Father," I replied.

"OK. Show me everything we have," he said.

I jumped up to open the study door for Father, then followed him to the library. X and two other men were waiting for us. Father was incredibly thorough. We went through all the data until three in the morning, and X and I had a long list of questions to follow up on.

Over the next twenty-four hours, we toured our other three major facilities in Hong Kong; we went through our intelligence two more times and updated the information every time new data arrived. Father said, "I want a full-scale attack planned on multiple targets for Sunday night. There will be no moon. Tigers hunt at night." X and I nodded as we looked at each other. We had four days to put the plan together and execute. That wasn't much time.

Piece by piece, the plan was slowly and methodically assembled. Two members of each of the two families were targeted, as was a major facility owned by each family. I ordered X to hire another hundred men. Failure was not an option. We rounded up two dozen moving trucks to transport all the men. This was going to be the largest operation ever in Hong Kong, with no close second. We would smack them with all our might. It also occurred to me that the family estate would not be well guarded that night, so Friday morning I texted the devil, "Assemble a plan to hit the White Tiger's estate Sunday night. Details to follow."

Later that day I assured Father that I felt responsible for losing the port warehouse, which was our second-largest warehouse. I told him I wanted to oversee the warehouse attacks personally and exact my revenge. He liked this idea. The minutes ticked by at a torrid pace as I barely ate or slept. Every possible detail was carefully planned. At 10:10 PM Sunday night, we would strike. At 10:15 PM, Father would get a surprise.

CHAPTER 11

Sunday quickly arrived. I got maybe an hour and a half or two hours sleep Saturday night, dozing off at the conference room table. I should have been exhausted, but I was completely wired. In that moment, I could see the remainder of my fragile life dangling in the wind. Would I survive the day? Would Father survive the day? I had my doubts about both questions but there was no turning back now. I thought of my angel Jessica and was envious of her innocence. A part of me knew that she was too good for me, and the rest of me didn't give a damn. I would do anything for her.

That afternoon I met a small army of men at one of our warehouses. Ten of the delivery trucks were inside, waiting to deliver us to the Red Dragon warehouse. X would lead the team from a second warehouse location that would attack the Black Serpent warehouse. I laid out a map of our target warehouse and went over the attack plan. The men were divided into groups and given their assignments. The team would go in while I and two men watched and directed from a distance. An extra getaway van was parked around the block from the target, with keys under the floormat. I had never been so incredibly focused as we rehearsed intensely, over and over.

At 9:30 PM, we loaded into the ten delivery trucks. There were fifteen of us crammed into the back of the truck. We were dressed all in black, with black ski masks resting on top of our heads. Three men in each truck had a gallon of gasoline. After the truck's back door was pulled down, two blue glow sticks illuminated our glowing faces as the truck's engine rumbled to life and shifted into gear. The energy inside the silent truck was incredibly tense as everyone attempted to make peace with their gods and loved ones. An eerie calm came over me as I realized that this was it. No matter what happened in the next hour, afterward I would not have to live a life as a person I despised. By 9:50 PM, we had parked, giving us fifteen minutes to try to gather our last thoughts, which slipped out like water between my fingers.

At 10:05 PM, the truck's engine fired up again, shattering the somber silence. As we began to move, one by one each of the men pulled their black masks over their faces. I'll never forget how only the whites of everyone's eyes glowed in that pale-blue light, and how those eyes said everything that could have ever been said. I and my two guards wore black baseball caps that we pulled down tightly, just above our eyes.

I turned on my walkie-talkie so that we could stay in touch with the teams in the other trucks. Three minutes later, our truck, which was in the rear, came to a full stop for me and my two guards to jump out. The truck's door quickly slid back down as all the trucks lined up, just around the corner from the target. Each truck had two gunmen in the front seat next to the driver. I walked quickly to the building on the corner. From the building's dark shadow, I peeked around at the warehouse. I texted Father, "All looks good. Going in." Then I looked back to our trucks and waved them onward.

The warehouse entrance simply had two guards out front with a double gate that was padlocked in the middle. Beyond that, a mechanical arm hung across the entrance, which would raise for cleared deliveries during the day. Our ten trucks shifted into first gear as the first truck came around the corner in front of me. I watched and heard its engine roar as it accelerated, with the other trucks in hot pursuit. Then the lead truck turned left, barreled across the street and crashed through the metal gate. The gate half-crushed and blew off its hinges as sparks flew from it, grinding along the asphalt underneath the front of the truck, which rambled forward through the mechanical arm. Caught by surprise, the warehouse guards stood up and watched in frozen disbelief as our next truck barreled in. Gunshots pierced the night as our gunmen quickly took out the guards, one by one.

A loud alarm rang out as our trucks screamed up to the front warehouse entrance. The rear truck doors flew open and our men streamed out. As they stormed inside, and immediately met a handful of guards, several more gunshots blasted outward. Moments later, sounds of a serious battle erupted as many gunshots echoed out from inside the building. One of the men must have put his hand on his walkie-talkie talk button as the sound of gunshots blasted through my walkie-talkie. I quickly cupped my hand over it as my two guards and I looked around.

After about two minutes, the pace of the gunshots began to slow down; then they resumed more sporadically as the team moved through the warehouse. The sound of sirens appeared in the distance. Our five trucks began to move around the warehouse to the side, near two dock doors that the team planned to exit from. Just then, Father texted me, "Abort! Estate is under attack. Get everyone back here!"

"Oh my God," erupted in my mind. I had been so lost in the gunshots and bloodshed going on in front of me, I had totally forgotten about the Chinese attacking the estate.

Everything was happening at once as my emotions spiraled up and down.

One of my guards said softly with excitement, "There's fire!" as he pointed. The fire alarm began to cry out from the warehouse with a different tune than the security alarm. I debated what to tell Father, and if I would really abort the mission.

I texted him, "OK." I knew there was no way we would get there in time, and I wasn't in a hurry. Then I got on the walkie-talkie and asked, "How long until we're done? Do they have any guards left?" I also texted X to see how his team was doing.

My team responded quickly, "Maybe only a few guards left. They are probably hiding or running away. We're in control and lighting the gasoline."

"Good," I answered. "I want everyone out in two minutes. Then we need to get back to the estate. It's under attack."

"What?" was the quick response in disbelief. Then a hurried, "Yes, Boss!"

"Let's get to the van," I told my guards. Just as we turned around, five teenagers came at us with knives. We had been so focused on watching the events across the street, we had become unaware of our surroundings. One of the guards turned just in time to take a quick stab to his upper left arm instead of his back, and he yelled out in pain as the other guard and I barely deflected attacks. My walkie-talkie bounced along the sidewalk.

"Our fathers work in there!" yelled one of the teens angrily as we fought. Luckily, I had Father's height so it was difficult for the shorter Chinese to get to me. One of them lunged at me with his blade. I sidestepped it and punched him in the face, stunning him long enough for me to land a second punch – which sent him to the ground as another knife slashed toward me. I jumped to the side, but the razor-sharp blade sliced a half-inch deep across my right shoulder. The fiery sensation of pain erupted as I groaned angrily, still focused on the fight.

He quickly came at me again, but my left hand caught the inside of his wrist just in time. Then I launched my right elbow into his jaw, knocking him straight backward onto the cement. The back of his head hit the sidewalk, so he would be slow to get up. I turned toward my two guards, who had their hands full fending off the other three teens. I caught the closest one by surprise, landing a punch to his temple, knocking him out cold. The other two saw him go down, then turned and ran away, quickly disappearing into the darkness.

"Boss! Boss! You there?" came the voice from the walkie-talkie several feet away. I quickly ran over and picked it up as the guards and I quickly surveyed our wounds. We were all bleeding, but nothing appeared to be life threatening. The approaching sirens were getting close.

"They're just kids," said one of the guards.

"Let's get to the van!" I ordered, and we burst into a sprint. "We're heading to the van. Get out of there now – the police are getting close," I said, with heavy breaths, into the walkie-talkie.

Just then, X replied that they had taken heavy losses but they were lighting the gasoline now. "Torch it and get out now," I said. "Make sure you're not followed and then head back to the estate. It's under attack."

"Shit!" he quickly responded. My heart jumped for a moment as I ran amongst the chaos, as it seemed that everything was going according to plan. I had given the devil the approximate security count of thirty to thirty-five men remaining at the estate. I prayed that his men would get to Father.

Back at the estate, the gun battle was raging as more trucks of men poured in through the front gate. The estate had a defense plan. Father was thorough. Guards knew which stone walls, windows, rooms or hallways they were responsible for covering, both inside and outside of the estate. The Chinese were taking heavy losses, but they far outnumbered the estate guards. It took them a long five minutes to finally breach inside through some windows in the front. "Hurry. They're inside," Father texted me.

"How far is it?" I asked my driver.

"Probably twenty-five minutes," he said.

"We're not going to make it," I said, as he braked hard to stop for a new red light. Suddenly, I felt sick to my stomach. I was bombarded with guilt and so many other emotions. Maybe I was human after all. I felt all my energy drain out of me. We really weren't going to make it. If Father was killed, I didn't want to see it. "If he survives…" I thought to myself. "He'll know it was me. There's no way I could hide this from him." I hunched over forward as my palms came up to hold my face. Ten seconds later I knew what I wanted to do.

"Change in plans," I announced. "We're not going to make it. Take me to the airport." Both men looked at me briefly, then at each other, thinking I was out of my mind. They were probably right. "It may not be safe for me at the estate," I said.

"Yes, Boss," the driver replied.

Then I texted our pilot, "How long until you can be at the airport?"

Luckily, he replied right away, "Thirty minutes."

"Meet me there and have the plane ready to go," I answered. "And turn your phone off now. I'll be there."

"Yes, Boss," he responded.

Back at the estate, the alarm was rung loudly as the Chinese attackers flooded inside. They, too, wore all black including ski masks, and their black bodies littered the hallways. Gunshots blasted throughout the estate and reverberated down the long halls. The estate guards knew where to crouch to catch the Chinese in a crossfire, but the number of estate guards was dwindling. The palatial estate was also massive, so finding Father was like looking for a needle in a haystack. Seven minutes into the attack, the faint sound of sirens appeared far off in the distance.

Father wasn't going to go down without a fight. He had crouched down in a doorway of a dark room with a view of the top of the main stairway. Another guard was in a doorway just across the hall from him. Three more guards were on the other side of the stairs. Black-clothed bodies were piling up at the top of the stairs, which eventually gave the oncoming Chinese some protection to hide behind.

Suddenly, two hands with guns appeared at each side of the stairs, and the bullets splintered the doorjamb as Father ducked backwards. Two more Chinese crept out from the stairwell as the gunfire from the first four pinned down Father and the guards. Father bobbed his head out and a bullet whizzed past him into the doorjamb behind him. He looked at the guard directly across from him, who was also pinned down. Father waved him backward as they both retreated into their rooms. The Chinese would have to come through those doorways to get them, and they had positions on both sides.

The move paid off immediately, as one Chinese stuck his arm and gun into Father's room and blindly fired off two quick rounds before the guard across the hall shot him in the shoulder blade, dropping him. Another Chinese shot into the guard's room and Father took him down similarly. Gunshots continued to ring out down the hallway toward the stairs and throughout the estate as the sirens sounded a little louder.

Two more Chinese quickly bobbed their heads into each doorway. Father and the guard both missed, as Father fired two rounds chest-high through the drywall. The Chinese on the other side bobbed into the guard's room again as the guard fired and missed. Suddenly, one Chinese sprinted past the doorway so fast that neither Father nor the guard got a shot off. Thirty seconds later, another one sprinted past them into position. Now they had a man on each side of both doorways.

Father and the guard braced themselves for the attack that would surely come. Time stood still as they gripped their handguns, ready to squeeze the trigger at lightning speed. They heard whispers from the hallway as Father's and the guard's positions were communicated and the attack was coordinated. Finally, a gun appeared on one side of each doorway near the floor and gunshots blasted out. As Father and the guard returned fire, the Chinese on the opposite side bobbed into the doorway, chest high, and opened fire. Father missed the first Chinese as the bullets whizzed past his head, but the second Chinese caught Father's bullet in the skull.

Multiple gunshots rang out from across the hall as the first Chinese peeked his head out and fired a few shots. Father dove to the side to avoid the bullets, got to his knees and pulled the trigger. "Click!" "Click!" "Click!" He was out of ammo. He popped his clip out, and before he could reload, the black-masked Chinese man was in the room, coming around for the perfect kill-shot aimed at Father's forehead. "Bang!" went a deadly gunshot, echoing down the vast hallway.

CHAPTER 12

Father's attacker reached his free hand up to his chest, feeling the warm blood where the bullet had exited, then he fell to the floor. The guard from across the hall had finished off his two attackers and then saved Father just in time. The sirens were near now, and there were a lot of them. Father reloaded, walked over to the doorway, peeked out, and then quietly stepped into the hallway. One of the attackers was on the ground, dragging himself down the hallway, smearing a trail of blood behind him.

"Turn him over," Father ordered the guard. The guard promptly flipped the man over and pulled his mask off, revealing a middle-aged Chinese man with short, salt-and-pepper hair and a beard. Father pointed his gun at the man's face and asked firmly, "Who's your informant?" The man laughed a little despite his pain. "Who is it?" Father yelled angrily.

The man laughed again, and then a look of sweet pleasure appeared on his face. "It's your son," he said.

"Bang!" went Father's gun in anger, and the conversation was over. Father stared blankly in the silence as the fangs of betrayal sank deep into his heart and spread their venom. Outside, the Hong Kong police cars arrived, one after another.

If I had ever felt sick before, nothing had ever come close to the feeling that jolted me when my cell phone rang with a call from Father. "You've got to be kidding me," I thought. "It cannot be." But the abyss in my gut knew it was true. I didn't answer the phone as he called me three times consecutively. We were just driving through the gate at the airport. Shortly a text from Father arrived. "Where are you?" he asked.

The time on my phone said 10:44 PM. "Oh my God. He survived. He's still alive," I thought. I was in utter shock. I ran my fingers over the handle of my handgun, readying myself to use it if I needed to. Father likely didn't know which two guards were with me. The pilot was already readying the plane when our car rolled up to the hangar.

"Father's alive," I told the two guards. "He needs you back at the estate immediately."

"Yes, Boss," the driver replied. It was good that they never asked questions. Soon, the two guards drove away, leaving me with the pilot.

"Where we going?" he asked.

"India," I replied. "I'd like to see Mother."

"Piece of cake," he said. "She's fully fueled up, so I'm ready to go when you are."

"Let's go," I said. I knew I was a dead man. I hoped for a chance to see Mother and ask her to somehow look after Jessica for me. I texted Jessica directly from my cell phone, which had never happened since I'd been away. "I love you more than anything I could possibly imagine. Thank you for everything. The only time I've lived in this life was the time I spent with you. You are my everything, my angel. Please pray for me. If you don't hear from me in the next few weeks, you know what to do. I will ask Mother to look after you. Don't respond to this text."

Since it was so late on a Sunday night, it did not take us long to get the OK to take off. As we taxied down the runway, I swirled and tumbled in a freefall into the abyss of despair. For a while, I contemplated blowing my brains out as I ran my fingers over the handle of my pistol. "I'm such a failure,"

I finally admitted as the plane's wheels lifted off the runway. "I don't even have the guts to do it."

The flight to India was several hours long. I was awake in a fog the entire time, dancing with all my demons, wishing things had been different. I had let everyone down. I had broken my angel's heart, and Mother's, too. I didn't think Father had a heart, but I imagined that cold, blackened and scarred thing cracking a little more.

The plane's wheels startled me as they hit the runway in India. Ten minutes later we rolled up to the hangar, as the pilot happily announced, "Quite a welcoming party today!" After parking and shutting the engines down, he came out from the cockpit and said, "My goodness. Are you okay, Boss?"

I was in a daze, staring blankly, as I strained to raise my eyes up to meet his. "I'll be OK," I said unconvincingly. "It was a rough night last night." He opened the door as two men rolled the short stairway up to the jet. I summoned all my strength and courage to stand up. I had to steady myself for a few moments, holding each seat's headrest on either side of the aisle. Then I trudged out of the plane, like a man taking his final walk down death row beneath a dark gray sky.

Twenty men were there to greet me, holding their hands on the handles of their guns in case I made any sudden moves. I held my hands up shoulder-high, then slowly reached down, pulled my gun out slowly and handed it backward to the man in front. I had no grievance with these men. Some of them I knew, and they had always treated me well. I was in no mood to fuel any more demons. I had surrendered to my fate. I just hoped I would get a chance to see Mother and ask her to look after Jessica before I met my end.

Not a word was said as I followed them to one of the black Mercedes and got into the back seat. The somber and silent car ride was soon over. When they escorted me out of the car, all the men were near the entrance to escort me inside. "All I ask is that I can see Mother," I announced as I looked at each of them. They escorted me to an interior downstairs bedroom with no windows or other exit. Exhausted, I lay down on the bed, hoping to see Mother before I saw Father.

I went in and out of strange, restless dreams. Many of them were about my strange childhood and Father. I dreamt I heard Mother's voice in the hallway, arguing with the guards. Then my heart leapt and I awoke, for Mother was indeed arguing with the guards. "I know what your orders are," she said defiantly. "I am in charge here most of the time. Do you want to upset me? What harm can come from a mother visiting her son? It will remain a secret." I sat up, then stood to go toward the door, when it slowly opened, and Mother came through.

"Mother!" I cried out, ran over and hugged her as tears streamed down my face uncontrollably. She hugged me back and cried, too. It was incredible how good a simple hug felt. There are no hugs in hell, and I had traveled long and far, down into the abyss.

Eventually, I calmed down and she pulled away just far enough to look into my eyes. "What happened?" she asked.

"I arranged to have Father killed," I confessed. "Apparently, it failed."

"Oh, noooo," she whispered softly as her eyes dipped to the floor. She knew, as well as I did, that Father was not capable of mercy, not even for his own son. She looked back into my eyes and asked, "For the woman? Jessica?"

"Yes," I replied, and the tears fell like rain again. It took me forty seconds to gather myself again. "I came here just to see you, and to ask if you would look after her for me."

"You are SO different from your father," she said softly as she shook her head. "There was probably no avoiding this."

"He left me no choice," I said.

She paused in deep thought for a little while. "I am not sure what I can do, but there's a pen and notepad over there. Write down her information for me."

I wrote down the information, and I gave her the numbers for my two men who had been looking after her. "These two men are also good, loyal men," I said sincerely.

Mother had gathered her thoughts while I was writing everything down. She said, "I love you, Nigel. I am proud of you. While you're still alive, there is always some sliver of hope. Is there anything else I can do for you?"

"I love you, Mother," I said sweetly. "So much." I pulled her in for another long hug. "This is all I wanted. Thank you." We hugged for about a minute, exchanging all the feelings that could be exchanged. Then she pulled away from me. She looked me in the eyes as she wiped my tears away. Then she turned and went to the door. Just before she turned the doorknob, she gave me one last sweet look. Then she was gone.

I felt a little better, having accomplished what I had come here for. Now it was time to simply wait for the end. Father was not one to waste time, so I expected him at any moment. I decided to lie back down and relive all my favorite moments, which were nearly exclusively with Jessica. I plunged into that alternate reality, and my tears of despair transformed into tears of joy and gratitude. Perhaps it had been a life worth living after all. I pondered how truly wondrous love was, how just a sprinkle of it could illuminate a life that I otherwise entirely despised. "Is love truly that powerful, or is it simply Jessica?" I asked myself and pondered further. How I wished to see my angel just one more time.

Somehow, I felt significantly better. Still not good, but definitely better. I had come to terms with death. My heart was broken for Jessica and for Mother. But I had also done a lot of very bad things. A lot of blood was on my hands. I deserved to die. At least I was escaping a life that I had been trapped into, a life that I hated. I was about to be set free. From the cell-like room where I'd been placed, I heard hurried footsteps echoing down the hallway, then the front door burst open. Father had arrived. I heard his heavy, always fast-paced stride as it rapidly approached. As I sat up and put my feet on the floor, I sighed and thought a quick prayer that he would go easy on me and put a bullet in my brain right here.

The door knob turned forcefully and the door flung wide open as Father steamed like a locomotive directly toward me. He stopped just in front of me, our toes just six inches apart. "Stand up," he commanded. I looked up at him for a moment, then I obeyed. There I was, staring eye to eye with him. My heart pounded relentlessly as his eyes burned through mine like a blowtorch. "You tried to kill me," he said angrily and matter-of-factly.

"Yes," was all I could say, as we continued looking each other eye-to-eye.

"Why?" he asked.

"I hate you," I said. Then my eyes looked away for a moment, then back. "You know why."

"Unbelievable," he said. Then he stepped aside to blow off some steam. "My own son!" he yelled, flailing his arms up angrily. Then he pointed at me and yelled, "I gave you EVERYTHING. You were a king!" He opened his arms wide with his palms upward, "All this. ALL this was yours. And you threw it away!"

"You gave me nothing," I said coldly. He stared at me in a silent rage.

"Nearly all of our men at the estate died last night," he said. "AND you nearly succeeded in killing ME!" He paused for a moment, then said, "You know you must pay for this." I nodded slowly in agreement. "Very well," he said, and the conversation was over. He turned and marched out of the room. Another business decision had been made.

I felt proud of myself for standing up to Father like a man, and I felt somewhat at peace with what was about to happen. But a good portion of me felt that I had failed. I let out an enormous exhale as I sat back upon the bed. I had failed Jessica. I had failed Mother. I had failed myself. I wanted to do so much good in the world, and I had only accomplished terrible things. I broke down in tears and prayed for forgiveness. I let it all out – every single regret and failure poured out of my heart in the next fifteen minutes as those scenes replayed in my mind. Finally, strangely, the moment passed. I found myself in an incredible silence, an incredible peace. All my life I had never experienced anything like it. It felt... divine. That's the one and only word that could describe it.

Suddenly, the noise of several pairs of loud footsteps approached in the hallway, and there was a booming knock on the door. The doorknob turned swiftly, and four men quickly came through the door as it opened. "You must come with us now," said Ahmad, the estate security leader. I could see both the seriousness and regret in his eyes.

"OK," I replied. I swung my feet off the bed and onto the floor. "Here we go," I thought to myself.

I stood up and Ahmad said, "Follow me." He was in front. Two of the men were on either side of me and one was behind me as I was led through the heart of the house and toward the back patio. It was then that I knew where we were headed. Soon we were out the back patio and turned left. As we walked toward the huge tiger pen, Father was standing there waiting for me with a few other security guards. One of them opened the gate as we approached. Ahmad led me inside as Father stepped in behind us. Then Ahmad led me to the metal pole, placed the shackle around my ankle and locked the padlock.

"Here's his blindfold," Father told Ahmad as he handed it to him.

"I don't need a blindfold," I said. Ahmad got a nod from Father and then tucked the blindfold into his pocket. I looked up toward the house. Mother was watching from her second-story balcony. My heart went out to her, having to watch her only son die a terrible death. She seemed still as stone.

Father looked at me with disgust, then he turned to all the guards and said, "You see this! No one defies me and gets mercy. No one! Not even my only son." Then he stretched out his hand, and a guard handed him the whip before stepping out and closing the gate. Now it was just me, Father and the white tiger. As Father stepped forward with the whip, I turned around to face my end with courage. At least I could try to not fail at this.

The tiger had been lying patiently in the shade of a tree, watching the table be set with her lunch. She looked me in the eyes, and she looked at Father. "Crack!" went Father's whip, a few feet in front of her. Her growl erupted as her mouth opened, displaying her long, thick fangs. I gulped, trying to maintain my courage as my heart exploded like fireworks, shooting electricity through all the nerves in my being.

The whip whistled through the air as it snapped again with a "Crack!" just missing the tiger's front right paw. She roared fiercely as she stood up on all fours and began pacing back and forth. Her thunderous growl rumbled as her eyes pierced my soul. Father gathered the whip one last time. "This is it," I told myself, and I braced myself to take it like a man.

The sound of the whip whizzed past me, and I watched it snap just in front of the tiger's face. "Crack!" In slow motion, her hind legs sprang her into a forward burst as she roared fiercely through her fanged teeth. In a split second she was before me on the left side as I watched her like a blur. She sprang into a leap and flew past me toward Father, who was safely behind the line. Her chain whirred as it extended, while I waited for it to stop her. This time, the chain did not stop her as her massive body easily knocked Father onto his back. Then she quickly pinned him down, with her huge right paw planted firmly on his chest. Father and the guards yelled out with terrible surprise.

Totally shocked, Father looked upward as he lay there. His eyes met Mother's on the balcony, and he knew who had done him in. A second later, the tiger took her long-awaited sweet revenge. She roared with incredible satisfaction, and it seemed to shake the entire earth. Then she turned her head and looked back at me. Her thundering growl rumbled as she strode slowly toward me.

I, too, was in shock at what had just happened. I braced myself for the end as she came to me, growled, and walked around my right side, circled me, then lay down at my left. I quickly glanced up at Mother as the secret she had shared with me played through my head.

CHAPTER 13

"Go in there?" I asked hesitantly in a high-pitched squeaky tone.

"Yes," Mother replied with a big smile. I turned and looked at the tiger. "Remember, she's chained up," Mother reminded me. "But even so, she would not hurt you."

I looked at Mother, then at the tiger, then back at Mother again. I had just escaped one death experience with the ambush in the car. "What's one more?" I said to myself and chuckled like a madman. Maybe Father was right about getting used to nearly being killed. "OK," I said.

Mother walked up to the gate of the pen, swung it open and gestured me to go inside first. I took just one tiny step inside, waiting for her to join me. She closed the door behind her and said, "Come." I followed her up to the line that marked the safe spot due to the length of the tiger's chain and stopped, but Mother continued forward, toward the tiger. About ten feet in, she turned, smiled and said, "Come" again as she gestured me to come with her. She seemed so calm as I stood there, contemplating my fear of being eaten alive. She smiled and gestured me forward again. I looked back at the tiger. She was still lying down, but she was watching us. She lifted her head. I could swear I saw her lick her lips just then.

"It'll be fine," Mother said reassuringly. I looked down at the line in the dirt that had been scratched through the grass as I took one small step over it, then another, and another. I reached where Mother was standing, when she turned and slowly continued toward the tiger. I hesitated, then followed right behind her. My eyes did not move once from the tiger's. I don't think I even blinked for fear that I might miss her spring toward us. But she just lay there as Mother walked right up to her, close enough to touch her. I was right behind Mother, terrified.

"They can sense fear," I reminded myself. "I must look like a juicy filet mignon right now."

"There you are, Tiraya," Mother said warmly to the tiger, as if she were addressing a sweet, young child. "How are you today?" Then Mother reached down and patted the tiger's head, then started scratching behind its ears. I about peed my pants. Then, suddenly, the tiger started to make a happy "chuffing" sound. My heart leapt, as the sound was so powerful and beautiful, and yet still I was somewhat terrified. Then Mother put both hands behind the tiger's ears to scratch, as she bent down and put her face just in front of the tiger's face, looking eye to eye. "You're such a beautiful girl," Mother said lovingly, as the tiger continued to chuff. She scratched for a while around Tiraya's neck, and then underneath the tiger's chin.

Mother continued this with her right hand, and raised her left hand toward me. "Tiraya, this is my son Nigel. Nigel, this is Tiraya." This close, I could see all the scars from Father's whip over the years. A sense of great compassion flooded over me. I could relate to her on many levels. The tiger turned and looked directly into my eyes as I held back the tears. I was frozen like a deer in her gaze.

"Come," Mother said to me. "She won't hurt you." I looked at her, and then back to the contented tiger. I exhaled and took a small step forward, and then a larger step, and once more. She could have stretched her neck out and bitten my ankle as I bent my knees and reached down for her. My shaking hand came down upon the top of her massive head as she looked into my eyes. Words cannot describe how incredible and exhilarating it felt to have my hand upon such a magnificent and powerful creature. It was truly, deeply and profoundly awesome as I connected with her.

"She likes to be scratched behind her ears," encouraged Mother, as she moved her right hand up behind the tiger's left ear to show me. I slowly slid my hand over behind

Tiraya's right ear and began to scratch. She looked at me, my face now just ten inches away, and chuffed some more as I scratched her ear.

"This is so incredible," I expressed to Mother with a huge smile as my stress released. "She is so incredible."

"Yes. Yes, she is," Mother agreed with a pleasure-filled smile. "She senses far more than we do. She senses your innate goodness. That is why she allows you near her. That is the only reason. The only way she might ever possibly harm you is if you threatened her, or if she was starving. And possibly not even then. I have been friends with her for many years now, while your father has been away. She is quite hungry now, as your father always instructs the staff to start starving her days before he arrives."

"No problem," I said. We continued to pet Tiraya and scratch her ears for several more minutes. Then it was over. When we exited the pen, I turned to Mother and said, "That was out-of-this-world fantastic! Thank you so much."

She looked at me seriously and reminded me, "This must remain a secret," she said. "Tell no one." I nodded affirmatively. Then we sincerely hugged again as she said with a huge smile, "You're welcome. I enjoyed it, too." Then Mother walked swiftly away.

Back to the present moment, I regained my senses as I looked up at Mother, awestruck with the realization of her glorious genius. I clasped my palms together, smiled and bowed a little with amazing gratitude. She was crying tears of joy as she smiled and waved back. I looked down at Father and saw the beautiful irony for him. For him, the most dangerous creature in the world had indeed been a woman – probably because he had always been such an asshole toward women. Two female tigers ultimately ended his time here.

I looked at Ahmad, who along with the other guards were still frozen in a bewildered gaze at what had just transpired. "I'll take the shackle key," I instructed him, as I held out my hand. His head shook briefly as he woke back to reality. He looked down at Father's body, then he looked at me briefly and then up at Mother before deciding to obey me. Keeping his eyes fixed on the tiger, he opened the gate just enough to stick his arm through and toss me the key. I caught the key, freed myself and knelt down to give my thanks to Tiraya, my face in hers as I scratched behind both her ears. Her powerful chuffing was so incredibly beautiful. Tiraya's chain had dragged behind her. I could see where one of the links had been cut.

"Thank you so much, you beautiful girl!" I said with heartfelt gratitude as I shared my affections with Tiraya. "I owe you my life."

I looked back at the men, who could not believe what they were seeing, and ordered, "Tell the chef to bring us ten pounds of raw meat on a large plate."

"Yes, Boss," one of them answered and he hurried off.

Soon, Mother arrived and came in to give me a strong hug, then she shared her thanks and affection with Tiraya. Tiraya's chain was attached to a thick leather collar, which I unbuckled. The beautiful tiger loved the feeling of having her collar off, and we scratched all around her freed neck. The men brought the plate of meat and set it down in front of us, which immediately got Tiraya's attention. That gave the men a chance to drag Father's body out of the pen.

"I want to set her free," I told Mother.

"Yes," she replied. "We'll just leave the gate open. She'll be fine."

It was widely known that Father had always kept a white tiger on the estate. His death was reported as a terrible accident, and we reported that the dangerous tiger had been killed. Tiraya now roams far and wide through the forested mountains behind the estate, but the chef always has meat on hand for when she visits Mother. The staff keeps a large metal plate and fresh water bowl always waiting for her on the back patio. In Hong Kong, where I would soon sell the family business for billions of dollars, the white tiger stood for power, wealth, fear and even death. In India, the white tiger symbolized enlightenment. I would call that a nice step up. After planning out the immediate arrangements with Mother, there was a phone call I had been dying to make.

CHAPTER 14

I couldn't hold back the tears as I walked toward my bedroom to call Jessica. I felt like I had passed through the fiery pits of hell and emerged, reborn, free in a life overflowing with love. I could not imagine a better feeling. I closed the bedroom door behind me as I pulled her up in my phone. I saw the text message I had sent her as I left Hong Kong. "I'm sure that didn't go over well," I admitted.

I wiped my eyes half-dry and then touched the video call button. It seemed as if forever had passed before I heard the dialing sound. The first ring came and went, then the second, the third, the fourth… "My God! I hope she's OK," flashed through my mind. Then, at last, the phone said it was connecting. A few seconds later, my angel finally appeared.

My first thought was that she looked like absolute hell. She was crying, and it looked as if she had been crying for a long time. "Are you OK?" she asked pleadingly.

"Yes, baby," I answered sweetly. "It's over. We are free now." I watched her tears of pain turn into tears of joy as her beautiful smile appeared on her wrecked face. "Even on the worst of days, you are the most beautiful thing I have ever seen," I told her, and we both cried in the beauty of that moment.

"I thought I'd lost you," she said.

"I did, too," I agreed. "It's all good now. Everything is good." I smiled lovingly at her and we both calmed down a bit. Then I surprised her again.

I knelt down, with my left arm stretching the phone as far away as I could, looking down at me from an angle. "I've literally been through hell," I confessed. "I did a lot of things I shouldn't have. I hurt a lot of people. At times, I was completely lost. But without fail, I would remember you. You were the one light that kept me going. The light that gave me hope. The light that guided me through the darkness when all else was lost. You are my angel. You are my everything." I paused briefly as I looked her in the eyes, then asked, "Will you marry me?"

She gasped with surprise and barely squeaked out a "Yes." Both her hands covered her cheeks as she said more clearly, "Oh, my God! Yes! Yes!" Jessica and I both burst into more tears. I felt a little bad for an instant when I realized she had been crying forever, and here I was making her cry even more. I figured she'd forgive me this time.

"I love you, Jessica," I told her.

"I love you, Nigel, so much!" she said. "I am so happy!"

"Me, too," I said. "You have no idea. I'm coming to see you right away." We talked for an hour and a half until I told her I needed to go and make the arrangements to see her. I gave Mother the good news. She gave me a huge hug. She was beyond happy for me. She, too, was now free, as she had always been required to stay at the estate in India. I also asked her for advice on my master plan. She said she would look into some things and let me know.

Thirty hours later, Jessica was in my arms. I knelt down and proposed to her again in person before we erupted into a hot mess. The feeling was beyond words. We both had doubted we would ever be able to be together. After all we had been through, now nothing was ever going to separate us again. A discreet beach wedding was planned in six months with just Mother and Jessica's parents present.

Meanwhile, Mother and I kept working on my master plan as I started taking flying lessons in the states. I had always wanted a pilot's license and to be able to fly a plane. Mother also bought a plane for me to fly when I was in India. I would go there for a week at a time and see Mother, and take lessons there, too.

The next six months were like a dream, and before I knew it, our wedding day had arrived. Mother and Jessica really hit it off. They were two beautiful souls cut from the same cloth. I will never forget how stunning and happy Jessica looked on our wedding day. Heaven must have needed sunglasses that day, she was so damn radiant. I never thought I could love someone so much, and that love just continues expanding. It is limitless.

We honeymooned for two months on a few secluded beaches around the world. We snuggled and watched every single sunset together. Everything was so beautiful. Our two favorite guards dressed casually and vacationed with us, posing as Jessica's brothers, to keep an eye on things. We always tried to be very discreet. All that was left now was to execute my master plan.

Over the following two months, Jessica and I traveled alone to visit five different beach locations. Each location was very remote, meaning that it had no established tourism or any reason for anyone in the civilized world to ever go there. They were basically small villages or rural areas around small villages. The cost of living in these places was minuscule, and we could grow a lot of our own fruits and vegetables. The place we liked the most was absolute paradise and the local villagers were very friendly.

A week before we were to go back to the states, Jessica awoke in the middle of the night, feeling incredibly nauseous. She threw up in the toilet and continued to feel sick and occasionally vomited over the next few days. We thought it must have been the water or something in the food, but she wasn't getting better. Finally, I took Jessica to see the one doctor in the nearby village. I was worried, and I especially didn't want her flying in that condition.

I was waiting in a tiny little reception area at the doctor's office when Jessica came out. She had a funny look on her face, a look that I had never seen before. "It's not serious, is it?" I asked cautiously.

"Well, yes, actually," Jessica said. "It's very serious." She gave me that funny look again. I was dumbfounded, and now worried. "I'm pregnant!" she burst out happily. I nearly fainted. As my vision was going black, I slumped over to the right side and landed a life-saving death-grip on the chair's armrest. If five gunmen had popped into the room and started shooting at us, I'd have been far more comfortable. But a baby! Holy shit. Wow. I did not see that coming.

"Woah," she said as she saw me teeter to the side. "You OK?" After I regained my awareness, I started laughing.

"A baby?" I asked, blinking my eyes. She nodded and rubbed her tummy with a huge smile on her face. "Wow!" I said. "I was not expecting that." I found my legs again, stood up and gave her a huge hug. "I love you so much," I said sweetly. "That is amazing! We are going to be the best parents ever!"

Three weeks later, the phone call I had been waiting for came. The timing was perfect. "I'll be right there," I told Mother.

The next day, I was in India. I had just recently earned my pilot's license there and was excited to do some night flying. I said hello to everyone inside the little airport as I stopped in for a quick bite to eat. Then I drove out to my plane, loaded a few things, started her up and took off. Flying at night was so peaceful and freeing. I really loved it. Thirty minutes into the flight, I was captivated by how beyond magnificent the stars were from up there. Below me, the area was very rural, near some rocky and steep mountainous terrain. Far below, I noticed a flashing blue light on the ground. I unpacked a couple of things and just then, my plane's engine began to sputter. "Oh shit. Here goes," I said to myself as my heart desperately pounded on the inside of my chest. I opened the door and jumped out into the freezing, pitch-black darkness, plummeting downward.

The icy air pummeled me as I accelerated toward the earth. I struggled to be patient as I counted to sixty, then I pulled the cord. "Poof!" my black parachute flowed out and opened, bringing my descent to a gentle glide as I headed for the flashing blue light. I landed poorly and tumbled. Mother ran over with a flashlight beaming at me, screaming, "Are you OK?" Thankfully, I was indeed OK.

I quickly changed clothes and put a cap on as we gathered the parachute and loaded things into the rental car's trunk. Mother got in to drive as I shut the trunk, then jumped into the passenger seat. "Glad you made it, Habib," Mother joked.

"Thank you, Mother. Thank you for everything. I love you so much," I said, as she handed me my new passport and identity papers. The local coroner had long been on the family payroll, due to the way Father ran the family business. I had been waiting for a body that was a good match for mine. I had bought two sets of the clothes I wore that day to the airport. My lifeless copilot had worn the matching set, including a large sterling silver belt buckle, and he was carrying my wallet, credit cards and IDs. The coroner would make sure the body in the fiery plane crash – and it was designed to be a fiery crash – was identified as my body. It was my plane. Many people saw me at the airport, so who would question it? Mother drove me for several hours across the border to the nearest airport. Jessica and I met a few countries away from our final destination and drove to our new secret home. No one knew where we were, and now that I was a dead man, no one would care to look for us.

We wanted nothing to do with a life of wealth and power. I had had more than enough of that. We simply wanted to be together, away from the madness of a society that has to constantly consume things, and away from competing power-hungry egos. Habib, my new identity, put a little money in a couple of bank accounts in the Caymans, and in one account in Switzerland. My plan was to never tap any of those accounts, but the money would be there just in case. Mother took over the family business. Only Jessica, her parents, Mother and the coroner, who now had more money than he would ever need, knew that I was still alive.

Soon our little baby beach boy arrived. We named him Kiran. Then, just eleven months later, our beautiful baby beach girl arrived. We named her Carly. I was blessed with such a beautiful family.

When Carly was just a few weeks old, I awoke really early one morning. I quietly rolled out of bed and went into the bathroom, closed the door and turned on the light. I looked in the mirror. I looked deep into my eyes. I didn't like what I saw.

I quietly slipped on shorts and a hoodie and walked through the darkness to the beach to watch the sun rise. I felt the cool sand beneath my feet. It squished between my toes as I stepped toward the surf. The fresh, crisp breeze gently blew through my hair as I sat down to watch and listen to the waves rolling in. Old feelings had been troubling me relentlessly. "I have everything I could ever possibly want in life," I said to myself. "Why is it that I'm miserable?" I confessed. I begged and pleaded for the answer as I sat there in the silence, meditating as my heart bled open. Images of my life began to flash before me.

I'll never forget that moment. As the sun slowly rose, it illuminated the clouds in yellows, pinks and purples. Then it illuminated me – and I realized that I didn't like myself. "Actually, I hate myself," I confessed. "I've done so many bad things. I feel I don't deserve any of this," I realized. I wondered if my family would be better off without me. Then I went deeper. I felt my guilt, and I mean I really felt it. Then I felt my hate. I felt my anger. I felt the abandonment from my parents not being around when I was a child. I felt my resentment. More than anything else, I felt the weight of all my self-judgment. As I brought up each of these emotions, I could feel them in my body. They overwhelmed me, and tears welled up in my eyes.

"I have everything I've ever wanted, but I'm stuck in the past," I somehow realized. "How do I let all of this go?" I asked. The tears rolled down my cheeks as I begged to be free of this unbearable burden. Then, a great dam burst inside as the emotions flooded me all at once. I cried so hard that I fell to one side. My entire body convulsed as I curled up into a ball. I had no choice but to surrender. I cried and I cried and I cried, and I cried some more. I don't know if I blacked out or fell asleep from exhaustion, but when I awoke, the sun was nearly at noon's height. My body felt as though it had been run over by a truck, but I felt so much better emotionally as I sat up. My tears had dried, with now-crusted sand on the side of my face. It was hard to explain, but I felt lighter, as though a great burden had been lifted. "Thank you," I said to the universe.

I sat there in the silence, overflowing with gratitude, wanting more. Memories of the old man with missing teeth, and his lessons on the keys to the kingdom, came to me with a greater awareness. He had once told me how a soul comes to this life with goals and lessons in mind. For the first time, I saw how the lack of love in my childhood was meant to teach me about love for others, as well as self-love. Then I saw the unconditional love that I gave and received from Jessica, Kiran and Carly. Like a punch to the face, I realized that all of the struggles in my life were what I had come here for. And once I truly had overcome them, oh what a life I would live. From this point, the greatest journey of all began. Deep inside me, I knew absolutely that the next two years would be intense. Every morning from then on, I woke up before the sunrise and went to the beach to let go of my emotional pains and self-judgments. I even learned to forgive myself – and later, to love myself. No lesson was more challenging or more rewarding. Mere words do not do it justice.

I also realized that my greatest teachers in life were Kiran and Carly. Through them I am having the childhood I never got to have. We play all day long, whether it's on the beach, in the water, wrestling or telling stories. They teach me how truly simple life is. There is only unconditional love without judgment, and no self-judgment. And with Jessica, it just keeps getting better and better.

As I learned to love myself, the love I gave and received grew so much greater. Jessica definitely noticed this, and welcomed it all in. The more I learned to embrace and let go of all of the emotions, experiences and self-judgment from my past, the more I became free – until finally, I had truly freed myself from the biggest asshole of all: me. I had thought that being free from Father and being with Jessica would make me happy, but I learned that true happiness can only come from within. The hardest lessons of all were self-forgiveness and self-love.

We are so hard on ourselves, judging ourselves in so many ways. Things happen to us – and then we hold onto them and beat ourselves up about them for the rest of our lives. This limits us terribly, like a prisoner's chains. But underneath it all, we are truly divine, eternal, beautiful, powerful and strong.

It is up to you, and only you, to break your own chains and set yourself free. I cannot find words that come close to how amazing this feels – and at times I am overwhelmed with gratitude.

Wise men have said that the moment we want something, we are no longer free. We so easily enslave ourselves. It seems that our very nature is to be slaves. I had all the money, power and sex anyone could dream of. I was a damaged, bleeding soul, feeding off other damaged, bleeding souls. My masters were cruel and so was I. I found it an empty and meaningless waste of existence. Father claimed to be a master of slaves, and in many ways he was. But ultimately, he himself was a slave to money and power.

All it took was one beautiful, awakened soul to pierce my heart and make it sing. That beautiful song resonated deep in my soul and became my everything. So throw away all the programming, and forget what others say you should be or do. Find the courage to face yourself. The key to your true happiness and all you've been searching for, simply waits within you.